JOURNEYS BEYOND THE PEAKS

an Irish Odyssey

from Despair to Hope

HISTORICAL FICTION

M.F. ERLER

JOURNEYS BEYOND THE PEAKS

Standalones

VOICES IN THE PAST

LAUREN'S DARK PASSAGE

FAR FROM MAGNOLIA DRIVE

AN IRISH ODYSSEY

THE PEAKS SAGA

Series

PEAKS AT THE EDGE
OF THE WORLD ~ *Finding the Light*

SEARCHING FOR MAIA

MOUNTAINTOPS AND VALLEYS

WHEN THE WORLD GROWS COLD

THE FOUNTAIN AND THE DESERT

BEYOND THE WORLD

WHERE ALL WORLDS END

JOURNEYS BEYOND THE PEAKS

an Irish Odyssey

from Despair to Hope

HISTORICAL FICTION

M.F. ERLER

AN IRISH ODYSSEY, *From Despair to Hope*
Journeys Beyond the Peaks
by M.F. Erler

First Edition April 2025

 FIRST STEPS PUBLISHING
Gleneden Beach, Oregon
FirstStepsPublishing.com

ISBN:
    978-1-945146-64-0 (hc)
    978-1-945146-66-4 (pb)
    978-1-945146-67-1 (epub)

All Scripture references are from the New International Version "Scripture taken from Holy Bible, New International Version (Registered Trademark) Copyright 1973, 1978, 1984 by International Bible Society. Used by permission of Zondervan Publishing House. All rights reserved."

All hymn texts quoted are public domain.

Cover Photo by Paul Erler, of Atlantic Coast of County Kerry, where my Irish ancestors lived.
Cover design and formatting by Suzanne Fyhrie Parrott

Please provide feedback
10 9 8 7 6 5 4 3 2 1
Printed in U.S.A.

AUTHOR'S NOTE

"The Lord is close to the
broken-hearted,
and saves those who are
crushed in spirit."
Psalm 34:18

In honor to all my
Irish Ancestors,
and to the millions who were
forced to emigrate, but
who with great determination
made new lives for themselves
and their descendants.
ERIN GO BRAGH!

Dedicated to all my Irish Ancestors especially
Thomas Cantlon and Margaret Crimmons Cantlon,
my great-great-grandparents, who immigrated
to America during The Great Hunger (An Gorta Mór.)

ACKNOWLEDGEMENTS

Thanks to Stuart James, our most excellent and knowledgeable guide on our Globus Tour of Ireland and Great Britain, 2022.

Also to Dr. Jon Hatch, Ph.D., graduate of Trinity College, Dublin for his most informative classes on Ireland, taught at Flathead Valley Community College, 2023-24.

The authors of the many books I read on Ireland and the Potato Famine, Irish Immigrants in Michigan and the History of the Michigan Copper Country. (See list in the bibliography.)

My father Robert P. Feser who first told me about his Grandpa John Cantlon, whose family emigrated to America during the famine. He's the one who planted the first seed, which led to this book.

To my Beta Readers for their input and suggestions:
Mary Schmidt, Retired Teacher
Pastor Tim Christenson, Colonel USMC (Ret.)
Richard Bartlett, LCPC, Ph.D.
Rev. Dr. Kurt Ziemann
Paul William Erler

BE THOU MY VISION

(An ancient Irish hymn translated into English)
Gaelic words by Dallan Forgail, 8th Century

1. Be thou my vision, O Lord of my heart;
Naught be all else to me, save that Thou art.
Thou my best thought, by day or by night.
Waking or sleeping, Thy presence my light.

2. Be Thou my wisdom and Thou my true word;
I ever with Thee and Thou with me, Lord;
Thou my great Father, and I Thy true son;
Thou in me dwelling, and I with Thee one.

3. Be Thou my battle shield, sword for the fight;
Be Thou my dignity, Thou my delight;
Thou my soul's shelter, Thou my high tower.
Raise Thou me heavenward, O Power of my power.

4. Riches I heed not, nor man's empty praise,
Thou mine inheritance, now and always;
Thou and Thou only, first in my heart,
High King of heaven, my treasure Thou art.

5. High King of heaven, my victory won,
May I reach heav'n's joys, O bright heaven's Sun.
Heart of my own heart, whatever befall.
Still be my vision, O Ruler of all.

FOREWORD

As related in the first two chapters of this book, which are based on true events, I have been to Ireland twice, and though not for extended periods, I have developed a deep affection for the people there. In addition, my father loved to talk about his Irish grandfather, who I think was his 'favorite grandpa'. We didn't know many details about Grandpa Cantlon, but now I think I understand, for I have heard several stories of Irish who experienced the Potato Famine, who prefer not to talk about it. In addition, there are other instances of great suffering and persecution that other nationalities have experienced in the twentieth century, which the survivors are also hesitant to talk about.

After learning more of the details of Irish history and especially the Potato Famine, I felt compelled to write this book because I see that some of the same things the Irish suffered in what they call The Great Hunger are eerily familiar even now, as refugees in our own times (the later twentieth and early twenty-first centuries) still face many of the same negative attitudes and prejudices that the Irish experienced both in their homeland, and as immigrants to new lands.

Many of the same political and economic attitudes are still present in our world. Events like the famine and the resulting Irish Diaspora have occurred throughout human history, and continue to do so. I hope that by telling this story, some will be awakened to the need to keep these histories from repeating themselves.

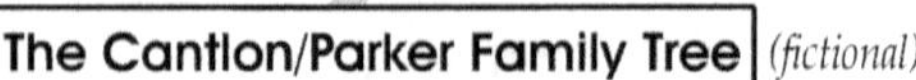

The Cantlon/Parker Family Tree *(fictional)*

Padrig Cantlon
dates unknown

Sinead Kelly
dates unknown

m. ? Ireland

- Patrick Cantlon *(b.1812 - d.?)*
- Unknown Siblings *(died young)*
- Thomas Cantlon

Margaret Crimmons
b. Ireland 1818
d. 1870, Canada

Thomas Cantlon
b. County Kerry, Ireland 1815
d. 1870, Canada

m. 1838

- Morgan *(1845-1847, Ireland)*
- Thomas, Jr *b. Ireland 1849 - d.?, Canada*
- Margaretha *b. 1850 - d.?, Canada*
- John Thomas Cantlon

Mary McLafferty
b. 1864, Scotland
d. 1935, US

John Thomas Cantlon
b. 1844, Ireland
d. 1927, US

m. 1882,
Michigan, US

- John Thomas, Jr. *b. 1884, Michigan*
  d. 1917, Montana
- Clara Maureen *(1886-1971, Michigan)*
- Mary Emilia Cantlon

Frederick Wilhelm Haas
b. 1887, Prussia
d. 1969, Michigan

Mary Emilia Cantlon
(1889-1976, Michigan)

m. 1910,
Michigan, US

William Victor Haas
(1917-2005, Michigan)

Florence Rene Parson
(1928-2015, Michigan)

m. 1950,
Michigan, US

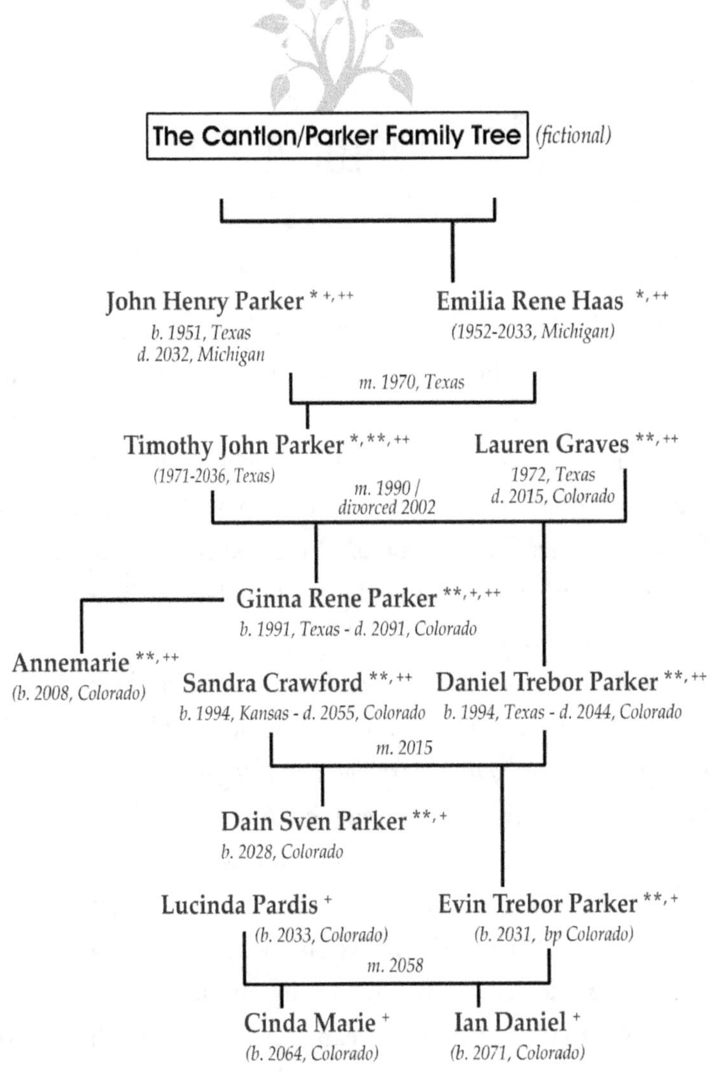

Characters are in:

    * *Far from Magnolia Drive*

    ** *The Peaks Saga* books

    + *Voices in the Past*

    ++ *Lauren's Dark Passage*

PROLOGUE

Cinda Parker was packing for college in the year 2082. This was the last box. In the other three boxes, she'd put her laptop, clothes, bedlinens and towels, a few small dishes in case she wanted to nuke a snack, and any other items she felt would make her dorm room seem more homey. This last box was for some of her favorite books. Print books were rare now, as almost everything had gone digital, but she still loved the feel of these old friends in her hands.

I hope I won't get homesick, she thought. Her younger brother Ian was keeping out of sight, which troubled her. *I wish he would just talk to me. He's upset that I'm going so far away—all the way to the West Slope of Colorado. I tried to tell him I needed more space of my own to figure out what I want to do with my life. But it must have upset him. He can be so touchy sometimes.*

She could still hear his words in her mind: "So all of a sudden, you don't want me in your life, huh?"

"No, that's not what I mean," she'd said. But he stalked out of her bedroom in the middle of her sentence.

Now, she wasn't sure what to do. She plunked on her bed, lying back and staring at the ceiling. *Why does growing up have to be so hard?*

She must have fallen asleep, for her room was dark when she opened her eyes. No, not entirely dark. A bluish light was steaming toward her across the floor. Glancing over, she expected to see her bedroom door open, but it was closed. Her pulse began to race. The last time this happened that GAP-crosser Lexi had been standing at the foot of her bed.

"Lexi, is that you?" Her voice quavered.

'Yes, Cinda,' said the all-too-familiar voice in her head.

"Why can't I see you?"

'Oh yeah. Here, is this better?'

The blue light moved closer, and soon, a long-haired brunette appeared beside the bed. Cinda sat up, trying not to shudder.

"I thought we were all finished with this time-travel stuff," Cinda sighed. "I mean, Dad is okay now. The only problem is that Ian is sad I'm leaving for college. Are you here because of that?"

'No. Actually, I didn't know about it. The problem is one of your ancestors again—actually more than one.'

"Oh great," moaned Cinda. "Again? I thought you got it all sorted out before, when you sent Ian and me back to Denmark, Bavaria, and Texas."

'This is also far back in time—a century or two. You need to go into your great-great-grandmother Emilia. She's married to John Henry Parker, the father of your great-grandfather Tim Parker.'

"I've never heard Dad talk about Tim."

'That's probably because Tim and his wife Lauren got a divorce in 2002. I doubt your dad ever knew his grandfather because Tim separated himself from the family.'

"Is that what I'm supposed to help with?"

'No, something even further back in time, maybe over two hundred years.'

"You're kidding, right? I've never gone that far back." Cinda brushed her fingers through her hair.

'Don't worry, you've crossed the GAP before. I know you can handle it.'

Cinda shivered. "Wait, it's been awhile. What is this GAP thing all about, again?"

'It stands for Galactic Antipaterminal Passage. It's a way discovered in the future, of jumping across and through the Space-Time Continuum. First-borns alone have the power to do it, though later-borns can be taken by a first-born, with some special help.'

"So I guess that's how my little brother Ian could do it, with that special help. And my dad told me his father, Danny, and his Aunt Ginna went with GAP-crossers Jon, Jael, and Martina."

'They were the first ones contacted by the pioneers of GAP-crossing from the Thirty-first Century.'

"How did you get involved? Are you from that future, too?"

'Yes. I'm Martina's niece. It runs in the family.'

"And after that, they came for my father Evin and his older brother Dain, who were Danny's children," Cinda shook her head, then spoke slowly. "Please, try not to overload me, but will you bring me back here when it's all taken care of? How long will this take? I mean, I start college in Grand Junction in a week."

'Remember, time won't pass the same here as it will in the Galactic Antipaterminal Passage, the GAP.'

"Oh yeah. So I guess you'll have me back in time for dinner." She couldn't help the sarcasm in her voice.

'Of course. Don't you remember?'

Cinda's eyes flashed wide. "Hey! I remember that last time

Ian messed something up—he erased our whole family line. Some strange hermit had to fix it."

'He was a Time Guardian. Don't worry. It won't happen again. We learned from that event.'

Cinda shook her head. *Can I really believe this? Maybe I'm still asleep, and this is all a dream.* "So, are you going to tell me what I'm supposed to do for this ancestor of mine?"

'It's better if I don't tell you yet.'

"Somehow I've heard that excuse before."

'I can tell you that you'll be in Emilia's mind, but you won't always be in direct communication with her. You will know when the time is right to communicate with her.'

"Lexi, this is scarier than last time. I'm not sure I can do it. Who is this Emilia, anyway?"

'She's your great-great-grandmother, remember? And don't worry; she will be open to her task when you explain it. She is developing a huge curiosity about her Irish ancestors.'

"Ireland? I'm going there?"

'Only briefly, during her visits there in 1970 and 2022. There, you will only know her thoughts, which will prepare you to guide her from the background, mostly unheard or seen. From there on, the task of being 'within' her ancestor's mind will be hers. I sense you're very worried.'

Cinda shoved her feet onto the floor and stood. "Well, last time you were there, at least part of the time. Weren't you there when I was in my six-times-great grandmother Elena? You were 'within' her sister Elka."

'That was your first time, Cinda. Now you're a pro.'

"Hardly!" Cinda paced back and forth on the brown carpet of her room. "I don't want to make a mess like Ian did last time."

'I told you we've got that repaired.'

"So you say. Why can't someone else go this time?"

'You know why, Cinda.'

"Because I'm firstborn, I suppose. And because I'll be in a female ancestor."

'See, you do know a lot more about this than you did last time.' Lexi moved close beside her and took her hand.

How did she do that so fast? Is she like a ghost or something?

With Lexi holding her hand, she felt a warm, calm seep into her. The GAP-crosser's voice filled her mind: 'Don't be afraid, Cinda. To start with, you'll only be back a century to observe some of Emilia's experiences. This will better prepare you to teach her how to Cross the GAP. She's the one who will be doing the hardest parts. All you have to do is prepare her for the task.'

With the warmth of Lexi's touch overwhelming her, Cinda took hold of the time traveler's other hand. They stood facing each other, and a golden light appeared between them in the air. The room spun around, but she wasn't dizzy. Then the floor seemed to fall away from beneath her feet.

'By the way,' came Lexi's fading voice, 'You will also be helping Emilia to go back another century or more into some of her Irish ancestors—'

"What?" Cinda gasped.

No answer came.

CHAPTER 1

Cinda Enters Emilia's Thoughts

The sign pierced my deepest mind: "England is Ireland's Enemy."

It was as harsh in its style as in its words, printed in black block letters on white, a sign framed and on a metal stand.

"That's not your usual graffiti," I said to my husband, John, my companion on this tour of Ireland.

"Yeah, Emilia, there's plenty of that in Londonderry's streets, even now in 2022."

He pointed to some colorful letters painted on a nearby wall. I couldn't decipher them. Perhaps they were in Gaelic.

As we walked along the city wall of Old Derry, our guide, Colin, pointed out where the wall had been raised and augmented by chain link fencing and razor wire. (Colin lived in Derry and had been hired by our tour company to show us around his hometown.)

"Below us," he said, "Is the Catholic neighborhood of Bogside. Up here on the other side of the wall is one of the headquarters of the Protestant forces. Why do you think they made this wall higher?"

"To keep the Catholics out?" asked a member of our tour group.

"Even more than that," Colin replied. "People down below would throw bottles filled with flammable liquid over the wall and into this building."

"Ah, Molotov Cocktails," someone else said.

"Yes," Colin nodded.

"I'm confused," I said. "I thought The Troubles between Catholics and Protestants ended with the Good Friday Agreement in 1998."

"I suppose you could say so in theory, but even now, each side has different interpretations of what that document means. While it ended the particular Troubles here in Northern Ireland, the sectarian differences between Ireland and England are deep-rooted. The history goes back to the English King Henry VIII in the sixteenth century. That was when Henry established the Church of England, the beginning of Protestantism."

"So he could defy the Pope, right?" said a woman beside me.

"Yeah, so he could divorce his first wife and marry Anne Boleyn," added a man behind me.

Colin smiled. "The strangest part is that both sides, Protestant and Catholic living here in Ireland, rarely attend church."

"So it's not really about religion at all—"

"Of course not," he said. "It's all politics and always has been. England has always considered this island a big problem ever since King Henry. One side commits violent atrocities, and the other side retaliates in the same way. The spiral never really ends, though, right now, we're in a period of relative peace."

"Except for the occasional Molotov Cocktail?" the man behind me laughed.

I raised my hand. "Which name is correct here—Derry or Londonderry?"

Again, Colin smiled. "If you're Catholic, it's Derry. But if you're Protestant, it's Londonderry."

* * *

The words of his voice faded as my mind slipped back to the first time I had been in Northern Ireland. It was 1970, and I was in the midst of a semester abroad program through the University of Edinburgh. I was just as far from my parents' home in Michigan as I was from the college I attended in Texas. One long weekend, I decided to go see Ireland, knowing from stories my father had told that I had Irish ancestors in my family tree.

Back then, the accepted mode of travel for students on limited incomes was hitchhiking, and this was how I got from Edinburgh, Scotland to Liverpool, England. I couldn't hitchhike across the Irish Sea, so I bought passage on an overnight ferry to Dublin. This way, I didn't have to pay for lodging.

When I arrived in the Irish capital early the next morning, I wasn't sure what to do next. Many friends in college had talked about the Guinness Brewery, so I went there for free samples. After a draught or two—or three—I felt energized enough to wander around seeing the sights. Following my usual travel pattern, I found the Dublin Youth Hostel that afternoon and stayed the night.

The following day, I decided to explore the Emerald Isle's countryside. It was only March, but temperatures were mild, and the land was moist and green, living up to its moniker. As I walked along the roadways, I held out my thumb each time I heard a vehicle approach. It turned out that getting rides in Ireland was quite easy. The people were very friendly and helpful. In one day I got all the way from the east coast of Ireland to the western side at Killarney, whereupon I found the Youth Hostel there, as well.

That evening, a rainy cool front moved in, and I realized I had only two days to get back to Edinburgh for school. I had no choice but to set out for Dublin again the next morning, walking along with my thumb out. I'm not sure what I thought I would accomplish, but I hoped my luck from the previous day would hold. Soon, it did. The second ride that stopped for me on my trek back from Killarney was a group of three young men in a small compact car.

"We're heading over to Kilkenny to visit a friend," they said. "He's sure to have a lunch for us. You're welcome to come along."

Some might say I was foolish to accept this ride with three males I didn't know. But in some strange way, I wasn't worried. *God has seen me safely thus far,* I thought. *I'll just keep following his lead.*

When we arrived in the town of Kilkenny, they drove straight to what looked like an old church. Parking the little car, they led me into the ancient-looking stone building. A man in a rough brown monk's robe met us in the hallway and exclaimed, "Ah, so good to see you fellows, and I see you've brought a friend. Come on in; I have a light lunch here to share. There's always enough for a guest." (Years later, I'd learn there was a deeply-rooted belief in Irish culture to help the stranger or traveler along their way, whether by food or other means.)

After our meal of fruit, cheese, and bread, the monk asked me, "Where are you heading today, dear?"

"I have to get to Dublin," I replied, glad he didn't ask for my entire story.

"Ah, well then, we'd best help get you on the right road," he smiled.

The next thing I knew, he was standing beside me in his long brown robe, helping me thumb a ride. With a monk beside me, of course, the very first car stopped. Yes, they were going to Dublin. As I climbed into the car and waved good-bye to my new friends, I couldn't help thinking it would be nice to have a monk along on future hitchhiking trips.

I arrived back at the Dublin Youth Hostel shortly after dark. Getting out my map, I contemplated how far I still had to go in only one day. Another fellow lodger was looking over my shoulder.

"You don't want to hitch in Northern Ireland," he said. "It's not safe like it is here. The Troubles, you know."

I was well aware of the Protestant and Catholic violence in Ulster in the 1960s, so I wasn't all that keen on visiting Northern Ireland at all. "I'm not sure I could hitch all the way from Liverpool to Edinburgh in a day, though," I said. "The ferry would take half my travel day."

"You could take a train from here to Belfast." He pointed at the route on my map. "There you could get on the Larne Ferry to Scotland. That would connect you with trains to Edinburgh."

This would be more expensive than I'd hoped, but it did give me a guarantee of making it back to my goal in one day. So the next morning I bought a ticket for the Belfast train.

Riding along, I watched the green countryside of the Republic of Ireland fall away behind me. Trains often travel through the bleaker parts of cities and landscapes, and this ride was punctuated by high walls with barbed wire and broken glass embedded in the tops of stone and concrete.

Once we reached Belfast, I was told I had to go to a different station to change trains. At an information desk, I asked the attendant, "Which bus do I need to take to get to the Larne Ferry train?"

"No buses are running," came the reply. "One was bombed last week."

My heart did a flipflop.

"You'll have to walk," the attendant's voice continued. "Here, take this city map. It shows you which streets to take."

My heart pounded as I took the map and set out in the streets of Belfast. Walking along one row of glass-fronted shops with barred windows, I happened to hear a low rumble. When I turned, I saw a huge armored tank rolling by, with British soldiers seated on top—their guns ready.

****

This was the mental picture I envisioned when I stood on the ancient city wall of Derry fifty years later.

As our tour group walked to the next stop, I told Colin about this Belfast adventure, especially the tank.

"How old were you?" he asked.

"Around eighteen."

"I find it very surprising that you'd do such things alone, and so young."

I shrugged. "Maybe I was foolish, but I was young and optimistic, and God took care of me."

CHAPTER 2

Surprise in Dublin

With the maiden name of Emilia Rene Haas, most people would assume my ancestry is German, but that's only partly true. My father's mother was one hundred percent Irish, which makes me one-quarter Irish on his side. On my mother's side, there are many English and Scots-Irish.

My Scots-Irish ancestors were Protestant Scots and English from the Borderlands—southern Scotland and northern England—to whom King James I of England, in 1610, offered free land in the northern counties of Ireland. This was done to create a buffer between Catholic Ireland and Protestant Scotland and England, and the nine counties of Northern Ireland came to be called *The Plantation of Ulster*.

King James' plantation of Protestants on seized Catholic lands wasn't the first, however. In the 1500s, Queen Elizabeth I had also planted Protestants in Munster, the six southwest counties of Ireland. My dad had said that our full-Irish ancestors came from this southern region.

According to the histories I'd read preparing for this trip to Ireland, English political attitudes toward Ireland as *The Irish Problem* date back to 1172, and Henry II, father of the better-known King Richard the Lionheart of *Robin Hood* fame.

As a result of England's policies, very few landowners were native Irish by the 1800s. The majority of Catholics in Ireland were tenant farmers, who relied almost solely on the lowly lumper potato as their source of food. When they could afford it, the family raised a pig to sell and pay rent to those landlords. In addition, everyone was required to pay a tithe of their earnings (ten percent) to the Protestant Church of England, a church the southern Irish didn't belong to and gained no benefit from. Besides this, England passed what were called The Penal Laws, which prevented all Catholics from voting, owning land, and many other basic rights. These were now only open to Anglicans. Other Protestants, like Presbyterians, Methodists, Baptists, and Quakers were also discriminated against; they were called "dissenters." Some of these laws were eased by 1800, but Catholics and Protestants were still viewed quite differently, especially in England, where the Irish Catholics were seen as lazy, primitive and even subhuman.

As time passed, these seeds planted centuries before led to sectarian violence that has lasted into the twenty-first century. The roots of the problem still haven't been fully resolved, but are simmering beneath the surface like a dormant volcano. The conflict has always been more about political power and less about religion, and the many plantations of people by English monarchs have borne much bitter fruit.

Four days after our tour of Derry/Londonderry, our tour group settled for two nights in Dublin, the capital of the Republic of Ireland. In 2022, it was a bustling city with a harbor on the River Liffey, which ran through the center of town. The old dockyards had been given a makeover into a pleasant pedestrian way, paved with gravel and concrete stones and a lane of shade trees running parallel to the riverbank. We didn't see any of the graffiti we'd seen in Northern Ireland.

The weather was perfect, not the usual cloudy and rainy Ireland I had known. John and I were on this trip to celebrate our Fiftieth Wedding Anniversary, which had been in 2020.

Of course, COVID had postponed it until 2022. We'd been married in 1970, my freshman year at Texas Tech. John was a year ahead of me, but we'd had a couple of classes together and fallen in love. We decided to marry at a simple Justice of the Peace ceremony, since I had the opportunity to go to Edinburgh University that spring. We married shortly after I got back, and our first child, Timothy, was born the following year. I dropped out of college to care for him, but insisted John finish his degree since he had only three semesters to go. Our second son, Tony was born in 1975, after John had graduated and found a job with an oil company based in Houston.

As we strolled along the tree-shaded Customhouse Quay, we saw a three-masted sailing ship moored by one of the docks.

(Photo taken in Dublin, Ireland by Paul Erler, September 2022)

"That's a beautiful sight, isn't it?"

"Yes," said John. "It reminds me of the tall ships we sometimes see sailing on Lake Huron in Michigan."

"I'm glad you agreed to move to my old home state, even though I know your heart is still in Texas."

"Well, after we moved to Alabama in 2018, we realized it didn't suit us. Even though our son Tony and his family are happy they moved there."

"Back in 2021, even though things were opening up after COVID, I just couldn't face going back to Texas, John. Not with Tim—"

He placed a finger on my lips. "Stop. Let it go. We're in your state now, and I'm beginning to enjoy the blue lakes and changing seasons. It's a good place. I do prefer the freshwater Great Lakes. The salty smell of the ocean always reminds me of dead fish."

We stared at the tall ship as we talked.

"It would be interesting to sail on a ship like that," I said.

"Of course, the sailing wouldn't be nearly as smooth as on modern cruise ships."

"I know. You're right," I nodded. "We've been spoiled by our two cruises to Alaska and Hawaii. Cruising was a relaxing way to travel, wasn't it?"

"Oh, sure. But I'm not ready to go cruising again until we see if COVID is really over and done with," he said. "I don't want to be stuck on a quarantined ship."

At those words *quarantined ship* my heart jumped and a sudden pain shot up the right side of my head. I grabbed John's arm and gasped, "Oh, no!"

I leaned harder on my husband, and he looked worried. "Are you all right, hon?"

"I think I'm okay now." I shook my head. "It was one of those quick dizzy spells I get. The doctor said it's connected to my migraines, or perhaps a side effect of one of my meds."

John gave me a long hug. "I'm sorry you have to go through these."

"Hey, it's okay. I feel better now."

By this time, we were standing right above the gangplank leading to the tall ship. A chain stretched across the entrance, with a sign showing prices and tour times. Printed above an archway were the words: *This is a replica of the Famine Ships, which carried thousands of Irish overseas during the Potato Famine in the mid-1800s.*

"I remember my dad talking about how his great-grandparents and their family came to North America during that famine," I said, looking down at the rough planking beneath my feet. "Those must have been very difficult voyages."

John nodded, "Crossing the stormy North Atlantic is seldom smooth sailing."

The ship showed no signs of life as we stood and gazed down at her. "They must not be doing tours today," I shrugged.

"Maybe they will before our group heads back to England."

"That's tomorrow morning, though."

John reached over and switched to my other hand. "Let's walk some more."

I took several deep, calming breaths as we strolled away from the ship. Soon, we came to some statues arrayed along the walkway. They were unlike any statues I'd ever seen. The first two we came upon were a man and a woman—each clutching a small bundle to their emaciated frame. Their clothes were rags, and their feet were bare, but it was their expressions that captured me the most. They had the most haggard features and haunted-looking eyes. The man was gazing slightly upward, and within the mix of fear and desperation on his face, I thought I sensed a tiny ray of hope. To his left, though, the woman's face showed only bewilderment and despair.

"I've never seen statues like this in my life," I murmured to John. "They look so forlorn and hopeless."

Two of several statues commemorating the Famine, by Rowan Gillespie, along the River Liffey on Custom House Quay, Dublin, Ireland, (Photos taken by Paul Erler, September 2022)

"From what I've heard of the Potato Famine, over a million Irish starved to death," he whispered. "Those who could manage left this island forever. Here, look at this sign."

A few paces beyond these first two statues, a placard read, "In 1847, the Earl of Tullamore evicted all his 120 tenant farmers, tore down their rough stone cottages, and left them to find their own way to Dublin. Those who survived the 100-mile trek boarded ships like the one moored here, hoping to find a better life in America, Canada, or Australia."

Just beyond the sign was a small statue of simply a pair of worn-out shoes. Near these, another placard displayed a map showing the road many had taken. It was labeled *The Famine Memorial Trail.*

I stood rooted to the spot in silence for what seemed a long time, until my husband spoke, "Are you all right?"

Turning to him in a daze, I murmured. "I've heard Dad talk about the famine and his ancestors' emigration from Ireland many times. But it never hit me until today what a tragedy it was. To think that the landlords refused to help their own tenants, and just left them to starve or fend for themselves—if they could."

"I remember a saying from one of my literature classes in high school," John murmured. "Our teacher often talked about stories that showed 'Man's inhumanity towards man.' This is a classic example, I think."

"Come to think of it," I said, "our tour guide mentioned a field we passed on the coach tour in County Kerry last week. He said it was full of unmarked graves of victims of the famine. No one even knows how many graves there are scattered across the country. People were so poor they couldn't afford coffins, and many were buried in mass graves."

"I've read that the blight which killed the potatoes was worst in the western counties, like Kerry," added John.

"I've done a little genealogy research," I said. "My Dad's mother's family name, Cantlon, comes from County Kerry."

We stood gazing at the sculpture of worn-out shoes, and a cool breeze began to whip the trees above our heads. As yellow leaves scattered in the autumn wind, I shivered, pulling my sweater tighter around my chest. "Let's head back to the hotel, okay."

As John took my hand again, he squeezed it and said, "We're lucky we have a warm shelter. The poor people that these statues commemorate had no place to go."

"And no coats, either," I sighed.

That night, after a rich and filling dinner, we settled into our luxury hotel room. As I stared into the darkness above me,

I tried to imagine what my ancestors must have experienced during the famine and their journey to America. What challenges must they have faced when they arrived dirt poor in the place they hoped would be a land of opportunity? Lying there, gazing at a barely visible ceiling, I decided I needed to learn more about their story.

It needs to be told and not forgotten, I thought.

Then words seemed to come from another voice than mine: 'In many ways, it reminds me of other atrocities and war crimes I've heard about. We must remember so these grim parts of history won't be repeated.'

Who are you? Am I losing my mind?

'No, Emilia. You're not crazy. I'm one of your descendants, and I'm going to help you go back in time into the lives of some of your Irish ancestors.'

"Wait! This is insane," I said aloud.

'I'll explain more once you are back home.'

No. This must be some weird dream.

There was no reply.

———

CHAPTER 3

An Unexpected Visitor

When we arrived home after our twenty-eight days in Ireland and Great Britain, the vision of those statues in Dublin still haunted me.

That statue of a man we saw could easily be my great-great-grandfather, Thomas Cantlon.

I began accumulating and reading any books that popped up on my internet searches about Irish history, especially the Potato Famine, what the Irish call *An Gorta Mor*, The Great Hunger. As I worked through the first seven I bought, I became increasingly appalled at the stories they revealed.

Over the course of almost a millennium, England had considered Ireland a country of barbarians, and there were many derogatory names for the Irish. *The Irish Problem* was a preoccupation of English Monarchs from the twelfth century onward. Some of the atrocities committed on both sides were so grisly that they sounded unbelievable.

One night, as I lay in bed trying to sleep, images of some of the things I'd read about Irish history bounced around in my mind. *Lord, I wish I could have been there to help those poor people. Or at least to see for myself what they went through.*

'I think that's what I'm here for,' came a voice in my mind.

What? Am I really crazy now—hearing voices? I thought you were just a dream I had in Dublin.

'No, I'm really here in your mind.'

I glanced over to see my husband sleeping soundly and sat up in bed, shaking my head. *This shouldn't be happening. Lord, help me!*

Then a bluish light appeared at the foot of the bed. Within its glow, I saw a face with piercing brown eyes, surrounded by a halo of brown curly hair. I covered my eyes to clear my vision, but when I looked again, the vision was still there. "Who are you?" I whispered.

'My name is Cinda,' said the voice I'd just heard in my head. 'I'm one of your descendants, born in 2064.'

"But that's forty-two years in the future. How can you be here?"

'It's called crossing the GAP, which allows us to jump across vast expanses of space and time.'

"I must be asleep and dreaming all this," I murmured.

The light suddenly disappeared, and I sighed with relief. Until I heard her again. 'You don't have to speak aloud to me,' said the voice that had called herself Cinda. 'I'm a GAP-crosser. I guess you could call me a time traveler. I think I've been sent here to take you back into your ancestors' lives.'

You think?

'Things like this have happened to me before, Emilia. Another GAP-crosser took me back into the lives of some of my ancestors. Now she's told me to do the same for you.'

I closed my eyes and lay down on my pillow. When I opened them, all I saw was the dim ceiling of our bedroom. *All right, if this is a dream, I'll go with it. And if it's real—well, I'll have to go with that, too. Did you hear that, Cinda?*

'Yes, I did.'

My heart pounded like it would jump out of my chest. *So am I dreaming or not?*

'Does it really matter?'

I hadn't thought of that. Maybe it didn't make any difference. "I don't know," I whispered to the ceiling.

'Just trust me,' Cinda said. 'To start with, I'm only going to take you back 50 years, into your past. Maybe you will remember this—'

Strange yellow and amber lights began flashing over my head. When I closed my eyes, the lights were still dancing around me. I felt like I was falling through the bed, then the floor, and then I floated in nothingness. My hands started to tremble. Soon the sensation filled my whole body. Just as I was about to cry out, my vision cleared.

I was sitting on a soft blue sofa in a sunlit room. Across from me was my grandmother, Mary Emilia, sitting in her favorite rocking chair. Grey hair framed her wrinkled face, but her brown eyes still had the twinkle I knew so well. Outside the window behind her, I saw the familiar Michigan pines and maples in her yard.

"So you saw Killarney," Grandma smiled. "Did you also get to tour the Ring of Kerry?"

"No, unfortunately, I ran out of time and had to get back to Edinburgh for school. Things I remember most, Grandma, are how green the land was and how friendly the people were. But in some ways, the country seemed empty. There were few houses but many ruins of overgrown stone walls."

"Ah, too bad you missed the Ring. It's a beautiful place." I caught a glimpse of tears in her eyes. "I heard a few memories from my father, John Cantlon, of times he spent there as a child. I even visited there once with my parents when they took me on a tour."

She had a faraway look in her eyes. "My father rarely talked of The Great Hunger." An uneasy feeling filled the room.

"The weather was dreary and rainy when I was there in 1970, Grandma."

"Yes, it often rained, my father told me. The worst was the bitterly cold winter of 1846, when it snowed for weeks on end. He said it was like one unending storm of snow and icy winds."

"Were you there, Grandma?"

"Heavens, no! I wasn't born until 1889, long after my parents and grandparents had made their way to America."

"When did they come?"

"I believe the Cantlons came in 1847. My father John was a child of only three."

"What was their voyage like?"

"I'm sorry, dear. I should have asked my father more about it, but he was too young to remember much. The main thing he said he recalled was feeling sick and hungry as the boat tossed and rocked in storms on the sea."

"I wish I could know what it was really like."

"Oh, child, those memories must have been terrible. Whenever I asked Dad, he would say, 'Those times are best forgotten. My mind recoils from them when I try to remember.'"

Shining tears cascaded down Grandma's thin, wrinkled cheeks.

"I'm sorry," I murmured. "I didn't mean to make you cry."

"Oh, I cry at the drop of a hat these days. I guess it's the price of having lived eighty-five years. Each morning I ask the Lord if I can go now—to see my dear departed husband Frederick."

I stood and moved toward her, taking her quivering hand. "I'm sure the Lord will take you home soon, Grandma."

She pulled one of my hands to her cheek. I felt the softness of her flaccid skin. "I pray God hasn't forgotten me," she whispered.

"The Bible says He will never leave us or forsake us," I murmured.

Her head nodded against my hand. "Yes, well, I'm ready whenever He is."

I stood there a long time, just holding one of her hands in mine while she pressed my other hand against her cheek. "I'm glad you got to see dear old Ireland," she said. "My father would have been very happy."

Then, the room around me began to swim and those amber lights flashed in my eyes again.

Are we going somewhere else, Cinda?

'Yes, it's time for you to see the Potato Famine for yourself.'

After all I've read, I'm not sure I want to.

'Admit it, Emilia, you *do* want to, deep in your heart.'

Yes, I suppose so. What year are we in right now? I'm all confused.

'You were just back in time with your grandmother in 1974.'

She died in 1976, I think. Are we going to my own time now? To 2022?

'No, we're going backward again. You will be 'within' the mind of one of your ancestors.'

At these words, my stomach churned, and I tried not to be sick. I failed, though. Soon I was vomiting into a stinking bucket.

CHAPTER 4

Crossing the GAP

Rough wood planks beneath my feet rocked so much that I couldn't regain my balance. I vomited into the bucket again.

"Where am I?" I gasped.

"There, there, Maggie," came a gentle male voice. "They say the voyages to America aren't always this rough, but winters are the worst."

"America?" I murmured. "Why?" As I lifted my head away from the smell in the bucket, my nose was assaulted by even worse scents—human waste and many unwashed bodies.

"Don't you remember?" the gentle voice said. "Ah—but perhaps it's the Ship Fever. It makes you forget, and some people lose their minds completely."

I turned to look at this man as he patted my back. He must have seen the confusion on my face, for he said, "I'm Thomas Cantlon, your husband. Don't you remember me?"

Then my mind opened like a door, letting in some light of understanding. "Of course, I remember, you oaf of a man." I hoped this sounded enough like recognition. Just then, the floor lurched again, and I fell into his arms.

"'Tis all right, dear Maggie. You just need to rest. Our son Johneen is asleep at last with Siobhan."

Thomas led me to a rough plank raised about three feet off the floor. It was just over a foot wide and the length of a grown man. With his help, I climbed onto what must be my bunk. A pile of soiled clothes was the only pillow, and a thin straw-filled mattress lay on the plank.

On the small bunk across from me, I could hear a child's deep breathing in sleep. I assumed this was 'Johneen.' He and the girl, Siobhan, had to share the tiny bunk because their fares were half of ours. My gaze moved to the bunk above them, where I saw Michael, a traveling companion we'd met on the road. After I was settled, Thomas climbed onto the plank that stretched three feet above my head. He had no mattress, only a ragged blanket.

Where am I, Cinda? Are you really in my mind?

'You're in an emigrant ship from Cork, bound for North America. It's the year 1847.'

But why?

'Because of the famine.'

Famine? Are you talking about the Potato Famine?

'Yes, but I think I made a mistake in bringing you to 1847. This is the middle of everything, the largest number of emigrations in a single year. It came to be called *Black Forty-seven*. I think I should have taken you back a few more years to when it all started.'

I sighed, but I couldn't tell if it came from my real self or from Maggie—or both. *Okay, Cinda. Let's get this over with. I hope it means I'll get off this wretched ship.*

As Maggie fell into a fitful sleep. I felt myself—the Emilia part—rise and disappear into those flashing amber lights.

Cinda's voice whirled into my mind—the same way as the colors I saw, changing from the warm amber to a harsh vermillion.

'Maggie Cantlon is your great-great-grandmother. Johneen grows up in America and becomes John Cantlon. He marries a woman named Mary McLafferty. They name one of their daughters Mary Emilia, your grandmother.'

All right, I get that. Why wasn't I put into my great-grandfather John? He's the one Grandma always talked about.

'Two reasons: He was born just before the famine, and he was only a child when this ship sailed. Besides, we are here to learn history,' the voice continued. 'And you can't go *within* a person of the opposite sex.'

I hadn't thought of that. So are you taking me farther back to when Maggie was younger, and to when the famine started?

'That's the plan.'

You'd better get it right this time.

'Don't worry, I will. This is my first time being the guide instead of the one being guided.'

Wait! What?

No reply came. Her voice faded like a gull winging into a fog.

The colors ebbed away, and the next thing I knew, my bare feet stood on green grass. It was day, but the fog was drifting and curling around me. My eyes made out a small stone cottage roofed with thatch. The man who'd called himself Thomas was gazing at me from the single doorway in the stones. He had to duck to come out, for the door was only about five feet tall. He looked much younger, and his brown eyes sparkled as he smiled.

$$\text{———}$$

CHAPTER 5

Down the Hole, 1845

I returned my husband's smile, now knowing who I truly was. I had no idea then that a descendant of mine was in my mind, though eventually, I'd learn her name was Emilia. Now I was Maggie—Margaret Crimmons Cantlon had taken up all the space in my mind. I was Irish now and understood the language of Kerry—the old Irish, which some call Gaelic.

As I moved closer to the cottage walls, I was pleased that the smooth, white sides showed how much love and care we'd put into this little dwelling. It looked like stone but was actually cob—a combination of straw and mud made into bricks. I had white-washed it this past spring, and Thomas had patched the places in the thatch roof that the winter winds had damaged.

Thomas drew me close to him and kissed me. "I've just returned from working the landlord's barley crop. How are you and our dear Johneen?"

I leaned against his firm shoulder, enjoying the strength in the arm that cradled me. "I was only looking over our potato fields from here. I made sure our son was asleep and safe."

"Indeed, he still is. But now that he's a full year old, he'll begin walking soon. Then he could toddle off."

"When he can walk, he will come with me."

Thomas smiled again. He always had a smile handy, and his brown eyes filled my heart with joy when he gazed into mine. I knew I was blessed to be his wife.

"Ah, but soon there will be another babe," he murmured and patted my ever-enlarging belly.

I snuggled closer into his embrace. "I'll manage," I sighed. "In fact, 'twill be better when I can carry this one in my arms instead of my belly."

With one last squeeze, he stepped away. "So, how are our lumpers doing?"

"I think we will have a good crop of potatoes this year," I said. "Every row and mound are full and green, so I'm sure the praties are filling out, as well."

"If they look good above ground, they are surely good below," said Thomas. "Soon 'twill be time for the first crop to be lifted, the new potatoes."

This would be our first fresh potatoes since last year's crop had begun to dwindle by early summer. To supplement the few we could eat, I often went down to the seashore and collected edible seaweed. My stomach growled just thinking about the fresh potatoes we'd soon get to eat.

Even as I thought of this, I felt our baby kick. I grabbed Thomas's hand and pressed it to my belly. "Can you feel that, darling? Our babe is happy at the thought of potatoes, too."

Another kick came, and he smiled and kissed me. "Not much longer until he comes, I'm thinkin.' It's already July."

"Oh, not until August," I sighed. "Why do I always carry the heaviest weight in the hungry and hot days of summer?"

"Perhaps you'll bear him at the same time our potatoes yield their first crop."

I nodded and leaned my head against his broad chest.

"You need to get your rest, Maggie. Go lie down while you can, since Johneen is asleep."

He led me to the back half of our cottage where a straw-filled mattress lay on the floor, our only bed. Our son's cradle sat beside it. I smiled as I remembered how proud Thomas had been when he showed me this wooden cradle he'd made.

"No sleeping on the floor for our wee ones," he'd smiled.

I looked at our first child curled in the small cradle. Soon, he would be too big to sleep there and would sleep with us on the straw tick. But then our next baby would sleep there. Thomas gave me a quick kiss, and I settled onto the mattress and closed my eyes. Then he pulled closed the piece of old muslin hanging from a rope across the opening to the front room.

"You rest while I get a fire going to roast a couple of last year's old potatoes," he said.

"Don't use the seed potatoes," I called. "We need them for our next year's crop. I did find some seaweed today when I took Johneen down to see the water."

"Don't you worry. We'll make it through these hungry weeks on one potato apiece each day. Then as August wanes, the new potatoes will be ready to lift."

His voice faded from my mind as I drifted into sleep.

Johneen's cries woke me in what seemed only a few moments. With a sigh, I lifted him from the cradle and put him to my breast. His loud sucking sounds indicated how hard he was pulling on the nipple.

"There now," I murmured. "No need to be greedy. There's plenty." *For a while yet,* I thought. *With the new one coming in just a few weeks, I need to start weaning you.*

As I sat feeding Johneen, the new babe began to kick again as if to say, "Save some for me."

This brought to mind something my granny had told me—that as long as I was nursing this child, I wouldn't conceive another.

"You were wrong, Granny," I mouthed to the warm, fetid air. Sweat began to drip between my breasts. With a finger, I broke the baby's suction and moved him to my other breast. *There's plenty for you now, wee son.*

Soon, I heard Thomas stirring the fire on the hearth on the other side of the cottage, beyond the curtain. "Praties are ready, Maggie."

"I'll be there soon," I called back.

When I rose and settled Johneen on my hip, I opened the curtain. There were our two stools in front of the open hearth. Between was a slab of old gray wood balanced across two stones. On it sat three very small potatoes. Thomas poked at each one with the point of his knife, and steam rose from them with a slight hiss.

"Three?" I said as I settled on one of the stools. Johneen tried to squirm free, but I held him firmly on my knee. He was too little to trust near the fire.

"It's so hot today," I sighed.

"Well, all we have is this fire to cook on—unless you want to eat potatoes raw." He dropped onto the other stool.

Then I realized why there was a third potato. It was for any guest who happened by. One of our strongest Irish customs was to always welcome whoever came to our door, stranger or friend, giving them some of our food.

In my mind I heard Granny's voice, "He who is stingy to the visitor will come to poverty in the end."

No visitor came that day, so Thomas and I shared the third pratie. I mashed part of my portion and mixed it with water and a little salt. Smearing the mixture on my finger, I got Johneen to suck and lick it off.

At first, he looked startled and pushed it out with his

tongue. The second time, though, he swallowed it and almost smiled.

"He's an Irishman all right," said Thomas as he watched me.

After we'd eaten all of the third potato, I looked into the dying fire. "If Granny was here, she'd scold us for not leaving the spare one on the warm stones, Thomas. She'd say we were tempting the bad fairies by not leaving some for them."

He laughed. "Your granny was full of those old superstitions."

* * *

As the weather grew to the hottest July I could remember, I wondered if we *had* offended the fairies or some other higher power. When relief from the heat finally came in the form of a heavy rain, we were relieved at first. But when the cold and damp continued for three weeks in August, we longed for the hot sun again.

The last week of August, I went into labor, just as Thomas was lifting our first crop, the new potatoes. It was a very hard labor. My first birthing had been much easier. I lay in agony for hours.

When Maeve, the Midwife, came at last, she discovered the babe was breach. "Little one wants to come feet first," she muttered. "He'll probably walk early and always be on the run."

There was much pain as she finally managed to turn the baby in my womb, so it could be delivered head first. This left me exhausted. I pushed as hard as I could, but it still seemed a long time before I heard the first cry.

"You have another boy," said Maeve. "Looks like he'll be a feisty one."

She put him to my breast, for I could barely lift a hand. He latched on quickly. Looking up, I saw Thomas peeking around the edge of the curtain.

"Come in," I murmured, catching my breath. "Now you can enter."

Maeve stood. "Yes, women's work is done now. Come see your son."

By then, I only had eyes for the wee babe suckling noisily. "He's hungry," I smiled. "You'd think the birthing was hard work for him."

"Sounded to me like you did all the work," laughed Thomas.

"Ooh, aye." My last bits of energy ebbed away.

"I think we should call him Morgan," he said.

"Yes, Morgan is a good name. I pray it's a lucky one." I laid my head back as Thomas kissed my forehead and wiped the sweat away.

Two days later, it was Sunday, and we took Morgan to the parish church in the village to be baptized. Father Coglin, our priest, performed the ceremony, giving our child his full baptismal name: Morgan Thomas Cantlon. My friend and midwife, Maeve, stood up for him as Godmother, and Sean, one of our near neighbors, was Godfather. The babe slept through the whole ceremony. I had no family because my parents and siblings had all died in the epidemic and famine of 1831.

People from the village came and shook our hands and admired our new little one. We had known these people nearly all our lives, for people in Kerry rarely moved. Sometimes, the men had to make the long trek to Dublin, crossing the Irish Sea to Liverpool to find work in the English factories during the spring. Right after the praties were planted came the *hungry weeks* as we carefully doled out the potatoes left from the last fall's harvest and waited for the new potatoes to be ready in summer.

This year's crop of new potatoes was smaller, so our *hungry weeks* seemed bleaker now. Father Coglin announced that he would ask the area farmers with larger fields to donate some of their food "to the Lord's poor and needy," as he put it.

I tried not to worry, but my heart was heavy as we made our way home that day. There hadn't been the usual feasting to celebrate a baptism because so few in the parish had any food to spare. A couple of single fellows had brought poteen—the strong liquor distilled from potatoes. I had no taste for it, and Thomas only took a few polite sips. The young fellows drank most of it and showed the drunken results of this most potent of liquors all too soon. This was when Father Coglin politely dismissed the celebration.

"I'm sure you all must be going to see to your fields," he said. "We pray the Lord will bless the later 'old potato' crop.

The priest did not mention working on Sunday, though some did when they had to. Yet, he worked on the Sabbath, being a priest, and as the summer wore into fall, he was always at the church all afternoon, giving out what food he had collected to the most destitute of our village. It hurt my pride when we finally relented and also went to receive our share.

Morgan turned out to be a colicky baby. He'd try to nurse, falling asleep before I could move him to my other breast. Then in half an hour, he started wailing again, fussing and pulling his little legs up to his hips. He'd nurse for a few more minutes and fall asleep again.

With so much trouble, I was glad that I'd weaned Johneen a week before my lying-in. Most of my days and nights were spent trying to settle Morgan down. I felt guilty that I couldn't help Thomas put the new potatoes in the storage pits. New potatoes had thin skins and had to be buried in a pit because they wouldn't keep as well as the later harvest of the larger, thicker-skinned old potatoes. Some of the new potatoes came straight into the house so we could begin eating them right away. I wished I had the time and energy to make potato soup or pancakes, for a change from always having them roasted in the fire. But Thomas insisted he didn't mind.

One late September afternoon, Thomas stalked into the cottage. "Give Morgan to me," he said.

"What? You can't feed him."

"Just hand him over. I'll jiggle him about while you get some air. Perhaps I can teach him to dance a jig with me." His merry face and sparkling eyes lifted my weary spirits.

"Perhaps I should use this time to make potato cakes—something different."

He shook his head and ushered me out the door. I stood in confusion until he took my arm and started walking, carrying Morgan over his shoulder.

"Come now, Maggie. Johneen has been toddling about the dooryard."

"What? Did I miss his first steps?"

Thomas didn't reply but called for him to walk with us. "Let's see if we can teach your baby brother to dance a jig."

Johneen toddled over with a giggle. Thomas held Morgan so his little feet dangled. Then he bounced him up and down. We both laughed when Johneen bent his knees and bobbed, too.

"That's my fine boys," Thomas laughed. "Now, Maggie, you need to walk around the cottage two times for your daily exercise."

The air outside did smell better than in the cottage. I stood and bobbed on my feet a few times before I left them and walked around as I'd been told. At first, that day had been sunny and warm, but when I came around the second time, a sudden chill breeze whipped at my skirt.

I walked back to where Thomas sat on an old log with the boys. "Ugh! What is that awful smell?" I asked when I reached them.

Thomas sniffed. "Smells like a stable that hasn't been mucked out for a long time. It comes on the east wind. Soon, though, it will rain and clear the air. It's been happening often this autumn."

Soon large rain drops plunged around us, and we all retreated into the cottage. I saw Johneen shivering and pulled him close.

"I'll stoke the fire and get more praties warming," said Thomas. He passed Morgan to me. I was surprised to see his baby lips turn up at the corners.

"Look," I laughed. "Morgan is smiling."

"See, Maggie, he enjoyed the outing, too."

From then on, we took advantage of any sunshine and went on a family walk. We expanded the walk to around the first set of potato beds.

Much too often, though, the sunny times were short, and drenching rains came almost every afternoon. Still, the walks were just what I needed. Gradually, Morgan settled into a semblance of a schedule as October began. The walks in fresh air must have been good for him, too.

One day, both boys fell asleep in mid-morning.

"Go out and walk around the plots, Maggie," said Thomas. "I think I can handle two sleeping boys."

I left our dooryard and walked the entire length of our potato beds. We only leased this half-acre plot to grow our potatoes. We could get many pounds of potatoes from this one small plot, providing much more food for us than if we planted oats or barley. Most of our landlord's land was planted in these grains, now ripe and shining golden in the autumn sun.

In a low grassy spot beyond our neighbor's potato plots, the landlord had a couple of cows and a few sheep. Such protein as meat was rarely available for us, though once in a while, Thomas had time to go out to the coast and catch a few fish.

With the green pasture still in the distance, I reached the beds of our neighbors, Kevin and Bridget O'Donnel. When I reached the edge, Bridget waved and came over to walk with me.

"Top o'the morning, Maggie," she said. "T'is good to see you getting some air."

I nodded. "Little Morgan has given me a tough time, but things are getting better."

"Ah, that's good," she smiled. "But the air is not always so fresh."

Just then, a strange odor drifted past me. "There's a strange smell on the wind today, Bridget."

"Aye, almost every day, it seems."

"What can it be?"

She moved closer to me and whispered, "Some folks say that the bad fairies are sending a curse. T'is an evil omen, I think."

No sooner had she said this than a cloud covered the sun. When I looked up, I saw it wasn't just a cloud.

"Look, Bridget, the whole sky has suddenly turned dark. What's happening?"

"It's the fairies, I tell ya. They're fighting among themselves."

Even though it was still late morning, it felt more like twilight. "I'd best be getting home," I said, pulling up my skirt and jogging back the way I'd come.

When I got to our cottage, Thomas stood in the doorway, looking up at the sky.

"Are the babies all right?" I cried.

"Both are still sleeping. Not to worry." He tried to smile, but I could see his worried glances upward. "This weather seems unnatural, Maggie."

"Bridget says the fairies are sending a curse upon the land."

He cleared his throat, as he often did when he poo-pooed Bridget's superstitions, but this time his usual laugh was absent. Then his eyes widened as he looked past my face at the sky. I turned my head to follow his gaze and saw a dense blue-colored fog moving in from the east.

"I've never seen a sky like this before, Maggie."

"That smell is getting to me," I coughed. "Let's go inside and shut the door."

Our cottage had only the door opening and one in the roof where the smoke from our fire escaped. We had no windows. Only the rich had such things.

Thomas stirred the fire and put on another brick of turf that he'd dried. With rain coming almost every day, it was impossible for the peat turves he'd cut over in the bog to dry properly. He'd started bringing in enough to keep the fire going, drying them close to the hearth.

He pulled me closer by moving the stools right together. "Don't worry over Bridget and her superstitions," he murmured.

"The awful smell is stronger than ever today," I sighed. "I don't think the door can keep it out." I laid my head on his shoulder. "It's almost as if death is outside, lurking at the threshold."

"Now, now," he whispered over my head as he caressed my cheek. "It's only the wind."

The room darkened around us as if it were night already instead of noon. Strange moaning sounds came and went over our thatch roof. But this time, no rain came. Then Morgan began to cry, so I rose and went behind the muslin curtain to nurse him.

Johneen had wakened. He looked up at me with frightened eyes. "Mama. Night?"

"Don't worry, Mama's here." I cuddled him with my free arm. "Morning will come back tomorrow."

As I cuddled our two boys, I prayed silently this was true. I heard Thomas's steps on our hard clay floor as he went out the door to get more turves to dry by the fire.

CHAPTER 6
The First Black Year, 1845

When I woke the next morning, I gagged on my first breath. The stench that had wafted past us the last weeks of October was now a hideous smell. Baby Morgan was howling as he never had before, and Johneen grabbed my arm when he saw me sit up. Tears welling in his eyes.

I looked at Thomas's side of the bed and found it empty. My pulse raced, and I tried to breathe through my mouth. *Perhaps this will diminish the smell*, I thought. It didn't.

When I picked up the baby to nurse him, he grabbed at my nipple fiercely. I gasped. Then Johneen tried to crawl into my lap and pushed at his brother.

"No! Ouch!" I cried. The shove had caused Morgan to suck even harder.

At that moment, I heard Thomas's steps enter the door. The slamming sound told me he was trying to keep the smell out. When he pushed the curtain aside, I saw shock on his face.

"I'm close to believing Bridget," he snapped. "All the potato plants in our beds have gotten black spots on them, and the leaves are drooping as if they're dying."

"Overnight?"

"It appears so. You didn't notice anything amiss when you walked by there yesterday?"

I shook my head. "Does this mean the praties will die?"

"I don't know." He shook his head and plopped down

beside me, laying an arm across my shoulders. "Some of our neighbors are already lifting out the second crop, the old potatoes."

"Well, they should be stronger with their thicker skins," I murmured.

He put his arm around my shoulders. "Lifting the potatoes now will give them less time to grow. They'll be too small to be worth it, I think."

I leaned my head back on his outstretched arm. "Do what you think is best."

"Aye, that's all a man can do." He stood and paced back and forth across the room. "I feel so helpless, Maggie. I have to do something."

"Perhaps go to the bog and cut some more peat?" That was all I could think of.

"All right. That's what I do today, but I might give in and lift a few potatoes tomorrow. I just don't know! Nothing like this has ever happened before. Maybe I should pray the Rosary more often."

"I'll do that for you," I sighed. "And after I get these two fed, I'll get some of the new potatoes out of the pit to cook for dinner."

* * *

The stench in the air got worse as the day warmed. Soon, I couldn't get Morgan to nurse, and Johneen fussed about everything. I finally gave up trying to feed them and hauled them both out to the new potato pit with me.

Morgan lay in a blanket near me. He wasn't able to sit up by himself yet, but he lay on his back, kicking his little legs. Soon he would be learning to roll over, so I kept him as close as

I could and made sure he didn't roll toward the pit. I managed to get Johneen to help pull the clay and reeds out of the top. He grinned when we finally reached the potatoes.

"There they are," I said and ruffled his reddish hair. "I'll reach down and get some out for supper." He tried to reach down, too. "No, dearie! Let Mama do that. When I lay them on the grass, you can look at them to see if they have any black spots."

I only said this to keep him occupied, but in my mind, I prayed silently that there would be no spots on these potatoes like the ones that had appeared on the plants last night. It was too far to lug the boys over to the potato beds, but I was afraid of what I'd see. By now, I knew that was where the stench came from—potato plants were dying.

When Johneen and I had a small pile of new potatoes on the patchy grass beside the pit, we looked them over. The first one he picked up looked fine, so I set it aside. Soon, a few more were added to this small pile.

"Mama—yech!" he cried suddenly.

I turned and saw a mess of black goo running through his fingers.

"Smells—" he muttered.

I reached over and turned the mess in my hand. It was a blight-stricken potato, all right. "We'll put this over in the bad potato pile," I tried to sound cheerful.

By the time we finished sorting what was close to a bushel of praties, we had three piles: the good ones, the bad ones, and a middle pile of those with some spots. Perhaps I could still use these if I cut out the black spots.

Before I took any into the cottage, I stuffed the reeds back over the remaining potatoes in the pit. It appeared that the ones on top had been the best, and the black spots and goo were deeper in the pit. *I don't know if any more can be saved. No, don't be a pessimist! Just make do with what you have, and let tomorrow take care of tomorrow. I think that's somewhere in the scriptures. Oh, Lord, please help us.* I didn't dare to say any of these things aloud, even though Johneen was still small. He was picking up words more and more these days.

I sent him to pick up the basket I'd set beside the door when we came out. He dashed over and carried it back with a big grin on his face.

"What a good helper you are, dearie." I smiled. "Let's put the good ones in this basket."

He eagerly grabbed the dozen or so potatoes from the good pile. Then he started to add the ones from the middle pile. "No, dearie, not these. We will need another basket for them."

"Room," he said and pointed to the half-filled basket.

"Yes, but a full basket will be too heavy for you to carry, and I have to carry Morgan."

He seemed to believe this excuse. I hauled the now-sleeping Morgan up onto my shoulder. *At least he's not fussing anymore. Maybe the fresh air helped, though it smells worse to me with each passing minute. Be careful now! You'll make yourself sick.*

Johneen tried to pick up the basket but couldn't lift it. "Here, son, you take one handle, and I'll take the other. See?"

This arrangement got us to the cottage door. It was still open so we could set the basket near the hearth. I laid Morgan on the blanket he was wrapped in, still asleep. "Now, let's put these potatoes in this pot." This was the only large cooking pot we had. "I'll go fetch the others."

"Me, too!" Johneen said.

"No, I need you to watch your brother."

"Oh, Mama—"

"This will make you my best helper, my dearie."

He made a pouty face but sat beside the sleeping baby. I took the basket we'd just emptied and hurried back to the pile of spotted potatoes, scooped them in, and ran back to the cottage. I wasn't sure what to do with the rotten ones, but after thinking a few moments, I decided I should keep them out to show Thomas.

Back in the cottage, Morgan was still asleep, and Johneen was curled beside him. With this opportunity, I started a turf fire and took the pot of good potatoes out to the pump, and filled it with water. I sloshed the potatoes in the water to get the soil off them. Then, I dumped that water on the ground and refilled the pot. There was no need to peel new potatoes for they had such thin skin. It could be eaten right along with the potato or slid off with your fingers. But I was disappointed to see the pot only half full.

I slipped back inside to check on the fire. Both boys were still sleeping, so I hung the kettle above the low flames. The smell of the peat fire helped cut the stench coming from the open door. I could have closed it, but I didn't. I knew it wouldn't help.

Now I pondered what to do with the spotted praties. I grabbed our wash basin and filled it with water at the pump. Then I sat on the stoop with my paring knife and cut out the black spots. These I tossed aside. I washed the good parts in the basin and let them sit on the stoop beside me.

I was halfway through the process when Thomas walked up. He pulled a low wagon with wooden wheels loaded with heaps of cut peat.

"What are you doing, Maggie?"

"Trying to salvage some of these praties." I sighed. "Did you see the ugly rotten ones I left by the pit?"

"Holy Mary! Those slimy black things were from our pit?"

"I'm afraid so."

"Did you get down to the bottom?"

"I had both the boys with me, so I couldn't. All I could do was recover the pit. I'm sorry." For the first time all day, tears began pouring down my cheeks. "What can we do, Thomas? If we don't have potatoes, we'll starve."

"I'm praying the next lifting, the older potatoes will be all right." He stooped down beside me and pulled my head onto his shoulder.

Now there was no stopping my tears or my dreads and fears. After what seemed a long time, I tried to get back to the job of trimming.

"Oh dear!" I looked up at my husband. "The ones I trimmed are starting to turn dark, too."

He took one from the water basin and one from the pile. "They all have a strange smell and feel squishy. Did you find any good ones in the pit?" His face had lost its ever-present cheer.

"There were a few. I have them cooking in a pot of water over the fire. It will make a small batch of soup."

"Well then." He tried to smile. "We will eat our dinner today with thanksgiving."

"But what about tomorrow?"

"We mustn't worry about tomorrow. 'Sufficient to the day are the evils thereof.' At least that's what they say, 'Tisn't it?"

"Is that in the Scripture?"

He shrugged. "I don't know. I just heard it a lot from my parents—when they were still alive."

He lapsed into silence. I could see he was hiding the shining tears that gathered in the corners of his eyes. Just then, Morgan began wailing.

I jumped up and dashed inside. He was lying on his back and kicking wildly. Johneen was just awakening. I picked up the baby. "I'm going to try to feed him, Thomas. This morning, he wouldn't nurse much."

"Don't you worry, Maggie. Johneen and I will take care of the soup." He sat down beside our son and gave him a pat on the back. "Won't we?"

Johneen nodded, still half asleep.

I already knew this thin potato soup would not be much of a meal.

If only I'd had the energy to grow a few carrots in our home garden, I thought. *But the birth of Morgan and his first fussy months took all my strength. And, of course, we have no meat because the landlord took our little pig this year as payment for our rent. How will I keep on feeding Morgan if my milk dries up?*

I shoved these thoughts to the back of my mind. Otherwise, they would affect my milk.

When Morgan was well-fed enough to stop fussing, I laid him in the wooden cradle. Now, Johneen slept on the straw-filled mattress with us. Thomas had spooned the cooked potatoes into three crockery bowls, covering them with the watery broth from the cooking pot. I noticed he took the bowl with the least in it.

"No, Thomas," I moaned. "You are the strongest. How can you work if you don't eat enough?"

"I'll manage, Maggie. After all, you're still nursing, so you are really eating for two. Now we must ask the Lord's blessing for our meal," he added.

This was something we always did, but today it was all the more poignant.

"Bless us, O Lord, and these Thy gifts which we are about to receive from Thy bounty, through Christ, our Lord."

Johneen was beginning to learn some of the words. When we crossed ourselves as we ended, I was touched to see him imitate my movements as we spoke: "In the name of the Father, and of the Son, and of the Holy Ghost. Amen."

With a sigh, I pulled up a stool and began to eat from the bowl Thomas gave me. Then he gave the third bowl to Johneen. The pot was empty. We had nothing to set aside for the stranger.

CHAPTER 7
The Famine Pot

Early the next morning, a pounding at the door woke me. I slipped out of bed as quietly as possible so as not to wake the boys. I saw Thomas already outside with his pitchfork, and I knew he just couldn't wait another week to lift the old potatoes.

But it wasn't Thomas who was standing at our door. It was Bridget.

"I told you, didn't I?" she began to shout.

"Shh! The boys are asleep." I pulled her several feet away from the house.

"Didn't you hear them?" At least she lowered her voice.

"Hear what?"

"The Banshees, of course. Night before last. They were howling and crying, 'Black potatoes! They are ours!' Didn't you hear their voices in the howling winds?"

"Well, the winds did sound strange that night."

"Aye, the day that darkness and night started at noon. I heard their voices clear as I'm hearing you now."

I stepped back, wondering if Bridget was going mad.

"You think I'm crazy, don't you?" It was almost as if she'd read my mind.

"No, Bridget. I heard the strange sounds, too. I think you are just more in tune with the spirit world than most of us."

She cocked her head and stared into my eyes. "Do you really believe in the fairies?"

"Of course I do, Bridget. But what can be done?"

Just as I said this, Thomas came running up from the potato beds. One look at his face made my heart skip a beat.

"Are the old potatoes any good?" I sighed.

He strode right up to my side and pulled me into a tight hug, ignoring Bridget. "We have to lift them all now. Maybe we can still save some of them."

"I warned you, didn't I?" Bridget screamed. Then she turned and ran toward their potato plot.

"What did she warn you of, Maggie?"

"She says the banshees were howling the other night."

"The wind was howling. That's for sure, a wind like I've never heard in all my days."

"She said they were howling the words, 'Black potatoes! They are ours!'" I burst into tears. "What can we do, Thomas? If the fairies are against us, there's no hope."

He hugged me even tighter and then massaged my back. "Don't let those old fools like Bridget and your granny drag you down into their superstitions."

I tried to nod. "But what if they're right? What if the fairies have turned against us? Maybe not enough of us are setting out the stranger's helping."

"We have to feed ourselves first, Maggie."

"What if the Good Lord is punishing us for our sins? Is this a warning, like the plagues He sent to Egypt?"

"We can work together," he said after a long pause. "I'll go talk to our neighbors. Perhaps we can salvage enough between us all to keep us through the winter."

* * *

Four houses were clustered together near ours, including Kevin and Bridget's. Ours was the only one whitewashed. The others were clay-colored and looked weary. Old Paddy's was leaning like the old man he was fast becoming. Our neighbors agreed to pool their stock of good potatoes with ours. There were thirteen of us, counting Morgan. Besides Kevin and Bridget, there was Old Paddy, who was alone now in his old age, and the family of Sean and Moira, who had four children. When my Thomas had gone to the last mud hut, he discovered it was empty.

"Didn't Moraigh and Artan live there?" I asked when he came back and told me.

"Yes, seems that I saw them back when we were lifting the new potatoes," he said. "On the way back, Sean told me he'd last seen them scrounging for seaweed on the shore."

"Where can they be?" My knees began to wobble as dark thoughts filled my head. "Could they have been washed out to sea by the waves?"

Thomas shook his head. "Anything is possible. I hear stories of people crawling into ditches to rest and dying in their sleep." He reached his thin arm around my shoulders to steady me. "God be with them, wherever they are."

"And God be with us, too," I sighed. "What have we done wrong to deserve this calamity?"

He patted my shoulder and took a breath to speak. I could hear the rattle in his chest, with him so close to me now. Then he just shook his head. "I have no words, Maggie."

The pile of potatoes our four families put together seemed so little that we cut out the black parts of the rest and added back in what seemed sound. The men lifted the lumpers still in the ground as fast as they could, but they were all small, being lifted too soon before they were fully grown.

Sean insisted on leaving one plot until the end of October,

when the old potatoes were usually raised. As the days crept by, we began to hear of many others in our area who had lost at least half their crop. Some had lost nearly all.

At last, we convinced Sean to raise his last bed. The men helped him while the rest of us each prepared a pot of soup in the largest pot any of us had. Mine was not as big as some of the others, but still, my soup mainly consisted of water and the few praties I could spare. We kept hoping we'd have some seed potatoes left to plant come spring. Moira's eldest girls, Maureen and Siobhan, went down by the shore to gather seaweed and anything else they found alive. They came back with just a few oysters.

Moira had a washing pot that could hold six gallons or more. To be fair, we decided to put all the soup into this one huge pot. My Thomas helped build a fire at the edge of our plot. Then he found a way to suspend the pot with three long sticks of hardwood and a large metal hook Old Paddy brought in.

"Where'd you find that?" Thomas asked.

"I dinna remember," Paddy shrugged. "It may have been on the shore, or perhaps my da left it in his pile of oddments."

I didn't care where it came from as long as it held up the soup pot. As I took a turn stirring, I knew it was still mostly water. Moira's boys, Mickey and Porick, each brought a handful of green grass and tossed it in before I could say anything.

Soon the other children were tossing in more grass.

"All right, that's enough," I finally said. "We're not cows or sheep here. Grass isn't our food."

Bridget came up beside me with a large wooden spoon. She dipped it in the pot and then blew on the liquid. "Well, it's hot, at least," she said. She took a small sip. "Here, Maggie, you try it, too."

I sipped out of her spoon. "Well, it's not too bad." I knew I was only making the best of things for the children.

"Can we eat yet, Ma?" asked one of Moira's girls.

"Soon, Siobhan," she replied. It needs to thicken up a bit more."

"Thicken with what?" I whispered.

Just then, Sean came running up the hill from his potato bed. Moira looked at him hopefully and then burst into tears. "They're all ruined, aren't they?"

Her husband nodded, gritting his teeth to keep from sobbing himself.

Out of the corner of my eye, a tear slipped down, and I saw that my husband had a tear, too.

"All I found was a mass of black slime," mumbled Sean. "You saw, didn't you, Paddy?"

The old man nodded. "I didn't have the heart to tell them."

"Well, I think this soup is as thick as it's going to get," I said. "Each of you bring a bowl or cup from your home, and I'll fill them with this large ladle."

As evening crept over the fields, we sat on the ground, each with our bowl of watery soup. There was maybe a third of the soup left in the pot.

"That won't be enough to feed us all tomorrow," I said.

"We'll get some more seaweed," said the eldest girl, Maureen.

"Maybe we can catch a fish or two," added her brother, Mickey.

***

Somehow, we four families made it through five weeks this way, adding bits to the famine pot that looked even remotely edible. By the end, though, some children complained of bellyaches.

As the autumn waned into winter, each family had to move back into their cottages to keep warm. We women made soup for our own family, and in a sequence, each of us invited Old Paddy to our cottage for dinner since he was alone.

Many days, my gaze turned to the ripe fields of oats and barley that our men were now harvesting.

"I'm tempted sorely," said Thomas one night as we tried to sleep on empty bellies.

"Tempted?"

"To hide away some of that grain for us. We do the work, and all the landlord does is charge us rent, then he sells his grain to England."

"Have they no charity at all?"

"I admit I would be ashamed to ask for charity," Thomas said. "But I think I should get something for the work I do for him."

"Why don't you go ask him?" I sighed.

"I don't think he'll listen, but I plan to try. Tomorrow."

<hr>

CHAPTER 8

The Landlord

I was so apprehensive when Thomas got ready to go see the landlord that I bundled up the boys and tagged along behind him. After a few yards he saw us and stopped. "Here, let me carry Johneen on my shoulders. He's too weak to walk this far."

It was true. We all were weak, for living on only a bowl of watery soup each day gave us little nutrition. Our skin was beginning to shrink as our bodies began using the fat and muscle on our bones to keep going. It broke my heart to see some of Johneen's ribs poking beneath his skin.

After walking for about a mile, we finally reached the iron gate that surrounded the manse's grounds. It was a tall stone building and had real glass windows with colorful stained glass across the tops—pictures of vines curling around leaves and fruit. My stomach rumbled at the thought of fruits I'd never eaten in my life.

If we had gone to the beautifully carved wooden front door, the servants would have shooed us away. We were fortunate to find the landlord, Earl Carlford, walking his dog in the grassy area just inside the gate.

He looked surprised to see us and curled his lips and wrinkled his nose as if we smelled bad. We probably did, for we had no soap for proper bathing. Besides that, we couldn't spare any of our turf for heating bath water. It was needed to keep us warm in the gathering winter and to heat the soup pot.

As we approached, he called to the dog, a deep-red-colored Irish setter. "Solomon, heel." The dog quickly came to his master's side. The landlord said, "Sit." And the dog sat on the grass. Both eyed us with suspicion.

"What do you want?" the Earl snapped.

Thomas set Johneen down and bowed low. I tried to follow his example, still holding Morgan to my chest.

"Please sir, we have no food. Our potatoes are rotting, even most of the ones we need for next year's seed potatoes. I work your land for you, but you pay me no wages. On top of this, you charge me rent for the half-acre I used to call my own."

"The King of England gave this estate to my grandfather," said the Earl. "You have no claim to it. The King's words are the law of the land."

Thomas grimaced as he replied. "This land was my ancestors' until you English shoved us aside. Have you no care in your heart for us, your tenants? We work hard for you, but you treat us like slaves."

The Earl's face was growing red. "You still owe me this year's rent. Besides, you're poor because you're lazy louts!" he hissed. "You spend too much time dancing, singing, and making babies." He swept his hand across the four of us. "And you are Papists, besides. Your Pope is not the authority here. I am!"

By this time, tears were trickling down my cheeks. "Please, sir, we just need a little grain to get us by until the new praties come next summer."

"The grain is mine to sell, not to keep up your wretched lives. If I could, I'd remove you from my lands and make more profit by raising sheep and cattle. Go to your priest for charity. That will keep him from causing trouble, the Papist!"

I wanted to shrink into the ground and disappear from his stony stare. Thomas picked Johneen up and put him on his shoulders. Morgan woke and began to fuss.

"Go feed your brats," the Earl snapped. "They are your responsibility, not mine." He turned away, calling "Heel!" to the dog.

We slowly made our way the long mile back to our two-room cottage.

That night, as I lay on the straw mattress, sleep eluded me. Then I thought I heard a voice in my head.

"Who are you?" I whispered into the chill of the night. "One of the fairies come to torment us?"

'I'm one of your descendants, always here inside your mind.'

I don't understand. I couldn't get my voice to speak now, and I shivered beneath our thin blanket. *Is it just the cold? Or that I'm so hungry?*

'I was told by the time traveler who sent me that I'm here to help you.'

What do you know about this famine? Is there any way you can help us?

'I'm sorry, but I don't know exactly how yet.' Her voice was wistful. 'Still, you are distant ancestors of mine, so somehow you survive. For I was born in 1952.'

Wait! Do you mean the year of our Lord 1952—in the future?

'Yes—over a hundred years in the future.'

Well, I suppose it's good to know that my legacy will reach that future. Your world must be prosperous and beautiful if people have found ways to travel back in time.

'I'm afraid there are still some of the same problems in my time as in yours. There are still poor paupers who the rich try to ignore. We know many more things than you, but it hasn't improved life. There are still some in my time who wonder where their next meal is coming from.'

So charity is unreal in your time, too?

'Not completely. Gradually, more people are realizing that we are our brothers' keepers.'

I've heard those words read from scripture, "Am I my brother's keeper?" Didn't Cain say them when the Lord asked where his brother Abel was?

'Yes, He did, but God already knew that Cain had killed his brother Abel. If it helps any, not all landlords here are as heartless as yours. Some are trying to help their tenants survive. Others don't live here on their estates but live on their lands in England. So they don't know what is going on.'

Yet you say some of this little family will survive?

'Yes, some of you will. Right now, all I can tell you is do the best you can for your boys.'

Are you like the others who turn away and expect us to help ourselves?

'No, of course not. I know that over in England, the Prime Minister, Robert Peel, is saying they should help you, though he's a politician like most and cares more about what people think of him than anything else. The majority in the Parliament don't believe the government should be responsible for helping you. They're much like your Earl.

'But in a couple of months, Peel will order some grain from America called Indian Corn, which is not controlled by the tariffs on other grains. Corn is courser than the gains here and takes more work to prepare. Watch for when it comes. I will help you learn to work with this strange food.'

Oh, thank you, I sighed. *At last, some help.*

'I can only do so much, Maggie. I cannot change the past. The time traveler told me it accidentally happened once and wiped out our whole family line.'

Oh dear, you are in a precarious place then.

'Fortunately, there was a Time Guardian who could repair that damage.'

This is getting too complicated for me. Just tell me when this new kind of corn will get here.

'I'm afraid that the wheels of government will grind slowly. They still do in my time, in fact. The Indian Corn will be ordered in November, but distribution won't begin until next March. You must find a way to survive this winter of 1845-46. I wish there were more I could tell you, but time has to flow the way it's intended to. Still, whenever you want to talk to me, I'll be here.'

May the Good Lord bless you. But what is your name?

'My name is Emilia. Your son John will be my great-grandfather, Maggie. I will do all I can.'

Her voice faded into silence. I noticed the night draw darker around me, as if there had been a hint of light when she was near. The strangled feeling in my chest and the hunger pangs had lessened. Perhaps talking to her helped me at least see a glimmer of hope for the future.

I was almost asleep when Morgan woke and began crying in his cradle. I quickly got him out and began to nurse him. My milk supply was dwindling, though. I wasn't going to be able to satisfy his hunger much longer.

CHAPTER 9
Making Do, 1846

Spring tried to show her bright face, but the weather was much colder than usual. With no fat on our bones and little muscle, we shivered our way through each day and huddled together at night in a desperate attempt to share the little body heat we had.

As the grass in our landlord's grazing fields began to green up, Sean came by one morning. "They're selling something called Indian Corn in the *clachan*," he said.

This was a small gathering place among the cabins and hovels of the Earl's tenants. I remembered this new corn was what the strange voice in my mind had told me of. Going back into our bedroom, I gathered one of the last blankets off the straw mattress and handed it to Thomas.

"Here, perhaps you can get enough for this to buy us some."

"You're sure?"

I looked down at my bare feet, then raised my eyes again to his. "Food in our bellies will keep us warmer than any old blanket," I said.

The *clachan* was almost two miles away, past the landlord's manse along a slender winding track. There were no roads to speak of in our area. The only path wide enough for two men to walk abreast was the one coming from the landlord's door to his gate, and there was a lane wide enough for wagons and carriages from there.

Sean and Thomas were gone so long that I'd begun to worry when I finally saw them trudging back toward our tiny huts, each carrying a grain sack on their back.

"Well, here it is, for what it's worth," Thomas said as he set it at my feet.

"What took so long?"

"I think all of County Kerry was there," he said. "Everyone clamoring for something to eat. You were wise to send the blanket. Most had nothing to pay with and were sent away empty-handed."

Tears collected in the corners of my eyes as I thought of those hungry people trudging home with nothing. "Is there no human kindness left in the world? Didn't our Lord say to help the poor?"

He shrugged. "I heard one of the men selling the grain grumbling to another, 'If we give it away, they'll just expect us to keep feeding their sorry asses. They're lazy enough as it is.'"

"Lazy!" I blurted out. "How can he say such a thing? Doesn't he know how hard we work for every bite we get? And that we must work for the landlords—"

Thomas put a finger on my lips. "Hush now, Maggie. There's nothing we can do but our best."

I was still quivering in anger when I heard that voice in my head: 'It's sad but true in your times, Maggie. The people who have food think the poor having too little is their own fault.'

We're not asking for charity. We try to make our own way, but sometimes, the merchants cheat us to line their own pockets. And then, of course, there's the landlord who would rather see us gone from his land.

'The forces of selfishness in my age are strong, too,' the voice added. 'Right now, I must tell you about this Indian corn.

It's not like the oats you are used to. It must be more finely milled.'

I have no mill, I sighed to myself.

'I know. You must cook it longer instead. Almost twice as long as your usual stirabout.'

"Thomas, open the sack," I said aloud.

He nodded, untied the string at the top, and poured a little into my cupped hands. "What an awful yellow color!" he said. "It looks unfit for man or beast."

I didn't reply but sent him to the nearby stream to fill my cooking pot with water. Once I'd poured the yellow grain in, I stirred it over the fire until it began to pop and boil. It thickened quickly, and the boiling bubbles sent globs of hot yellow goo onto my hands as I tried to stir.

"I think we need more water, Thomas."

He hurried down and returned with some in our only two crockery cups. "Is it ready yet? It seems like it should be."

I shook my head. "This grain won't soften like oats. It has to cook longer."

"How do you know this?"

"I'm not sure," I lied. "Somehow, I can tell by how it feels as I stir."

He glanced askance at me, then shrugged and walked away. "I'll tell Kevin and Bridget to come share with us," he said over his shoulder. "Sean was going to get Old Paddy."

While I was still watching my pot of Indian corn stirabout, Sean and his family, with Old Paddy, were already seated on the ground nearby, wolfing down the yellow mush.

"Isn't it ready yet?" Bridget asked when she walked up to me.

I shook my head. "It needs a bit longer, I think."

Are you here, Emilia? I thought to myself. *You said I could talk to you when I needed to.*

'Yes, I'm still here in your mind, Maggie.'

Well, is this ready or not? The yellow color looks wicked. How can we be sure it isn't a plot from the English to kill us off while pretending to feed us?

'Old Robert Peel means well. He has to deal with English merchants who want to keep their profits in other grains. This is the only one that doesn't have tariffs or import restrictions.'

How can you know all this? What are tariffs, anyway?

'Never mind, Maggie. Like I said, there are things I can't change, but I'm here to make sure you go on living somehow. Otherwise, my family and I will never be born.'

I shuddered. Why was I trusting a strange voice like this? Perhaps it was one of the fairies come to deceive me. But what other hope did we have anyway?

'I think it's cooked enough now,' came the voice as I shuddered again.

Even though our stomachs were growling, we ate the strange yellow mush carefully. It was gritty between our teeth—not at all like the oats we used to get when times were better.

That night, we all slept better than we had for some weeks. But the next morning, Moira came by shaking her head.

"I've heard people call that evil yellow stuff Peal's Brimstone," she snapped. "It's given three of my children the bloody flux. What about you?"

"We are all doing okay," I said. "I noticed that I cooked mine longer than you did. Perhaps you should try that."

"Oh, ach!" she threw up her hands. "How am I supposed to tell my starving children to wait while it cooks so long?"

Before I could answer, she stalked away. Later in the day, though, I did see her standing by a fire Sean had lit outside their door, stirring and waiting, letting the mush cook much longer.

* * *

With the Indian corn, we managed to get through the planting season. Thomas had to buy more so we could manage until the new potatoes could be raised. He sold his coat this time.

"Hey, it's spring," he said. "What do I need a coat for?"

I knew he was trying to sound hopeful for Johneen's sake.

We all felt hopeful as we planted the seed potatoes in the raised furrows of what was called our "Lazy Beds." They were called this because they sloped into the side of small rises between bogs or ground too rough for the landlord to claim for his grain fields. After what the Earl had said, though, I found I didn't like the name. It reminded me of how he'd told us we were poor because we were lazy. Whenever I heard his words echo in my mind, my blood began to boil. *Lazy, indeed! He's the lazy one sitting there in his posh manse while we do his work for free.*

Yes, we'd been so hopeful, but when the summer raising came around for the new potatoes, our hearts were broken. There were even more black potatoes this year than in '45. Even when our neighbors added theirs to the pile, it was only half as big as last year's. We had to go back to sharing the famine pot, and this year, I let the children add as much grass as they wanted. It seemed even this grass was blighted now, for it turned brown sooner than it should.

One night, just before it was time to raise the 'old potatoes' in October, I felt Thomas slip out of the bed beside me.

"Where on earth are you going?" I mumbled.

"Don't ask," he whispered. "Sean and I have a plan. The less you know right now, the better."

I lay staring into the dark the whole time he was gone, trying to keep my breath slow and my heart from racing. At last, shortly before sunrise, I heard him slip in the cottage door.

Crawling out of bed, I met him and saw he was carrying a large pail.

"What's that, Thomas?"

"Shh! Don't wake the boys. It's for the famine pot."

He pushed me back through the curtain and pulled me into bed. When I tried to speak, he kept his finger on my lips.

Once daylight came, I slipped out from under his outstretched arm without waking him. I stared into the pail and saw it was full of a dark red liquid. By the smell, I knew right away what it was.

"What on earth?" I couldn't keep myself from speaking aloud.

He was quickly at my side. "Don't worry, Maggie. This will give us more nutrition than we've had in a long time. We milked one of the Earl's cattle."

"This isn't milk! What have you done?"

He pulled me out the door so we could talk. "Don't worry, we didn't kill anything. Sean has taught me how to corner one of the cows or steers and make a small cut in its neck where we can drain some blood from one of the veins. We only take a couple of buckets full and let the beast go."

"But what if the Earl finds out?" I felt my hands and arms begin to shake. My head whirled, and I stumbled into Thomas.

He wrapped his lean arms around me. "Sean says a fella from across the way, on the other side of the clachan, told him about it. No one has ever noticed."

I was too weak and dizzy to reply.

Soon, Johneen came out to join us. "What's the smelly stuff in the pail?" he asked.

"Something that will help you grow," said Thomas.

"Aak!" came a cry from just inside the door.

I rushed in and pulled Morgan away from the pail. He was barely walking, and his tottering threatened to spill the pail's contents.

"Never you mind," I said, trying my best to sound cheerful. "It will all be fine once it's in the soup."

From then on the soup in the famine pot had a deep reddish brown color. No one said anything about it, and we did feel a little less hungry when the soup had that hue. I pretended to myself that the blood was actually gravy.

Heartbreak came again with the October lifting of the lumpers. Very few were sound, and there was nothing we could do but dole them out into the famine pot.

"What about saving some for seed potatoes?" Moira asked once.

"What good will seed potatoes do if we all are dead of starvation come spring?" snapped Sean.

Thomas only nodded and looked away from me.

CHAPTER 10
The Terrible Winter of 46-47

Wintry winds came early that fall, and we were told there would be no more grain sales. Sean said he'd heard that Peel was out as Prime Minister, and the new one, Lord John Russell, disapproved of selling us corn. By November, our ground was covered with snow, and I regretted selling our blanket. Thomas never complained about the loss of his coat, but I could see him shivering when he thought I wasn't looking.

The famine pots became mostly water and grass, with occasional mussels or seaweed. Then it was too cold for us to gather outdoors with our neighbors, and each family retreated to its own hut. Peat fires smoked through the hole in each roof, but I knew the others were just like us, with nothing to cook on the fires. We were just huddled around them for the little heat they could give.

Soon the boys came down with fevers and dysentery. When the flux hit me, I was too weak to clean myself, let alone them. While the winter winds roared outside, we lay in our own filth. I could hear Morgan whimpering, and tried to nurse him, but my milk had gone dry. I had too little flesh left on my bones.

As the snow piled ever higher outside the door, I lay on our smelly straw mattress and wondered if I heard banshees, the harbingers of death, in the wind. My mind drifted in and out of delirium. Sometimes I heard my old granny telling her tales of long ago:

"Long ages ago, before any of my grandsires were born, the *Tuatha de Dannan*, the People of Danu, came from out of the east, far beyond the world we now know. Some say they were on the very eastern edge of Europe. They had lived beside a river which was named for them—a name it still carries to this day. They were deeply spiritual people and could speak with the trees, the beasts, and the waters. Then a new people, the Milesians, came from the east, and pushed them westwards. The Tuatha de Dannan made a pact with them. They would let the new people have the land above the ground, and the People of Danu would take the part of the world below the ground. Even today, if you look and listen carefully, you may hear one of them singing in a bubbling spring or speaking from the ground at the roots of one of the great oaks. Alas, most of the oaks are gone now, cut down to build English ships.

"Then more people came out of the east, and again the natives of this land were pushed west. This time, they were called Norsemen. They arrived in longships of fine wood with dragon heads on the prows. Their desire was gold and land. They built cities along the coasts and soon became part of the land and its people. But after them came another race called the Normans, and though they were descended from the Norse, they were not like them. A few hundred years had passed, and these new people took joy in building great castles of stone. Those who had wealth subjected the poor to farm their lands for them. In return they promised to provide defense from enemies. For some time, they did. But many of the native people moved farther west again to try and live as they had for centuries before. They did not want cities with high stone walls or knights with their mighty horses. Their desires were for villages with their families, freedom to live by their old laws, and to care for one another instead of depending on some nobleman's promises.

"Ah yes, my dear Maggie, this has been the tale of our people for time immemorial. Another tribe comes into our land from the east, and we are pushed farther west. After the Normans came their offspring, the English. They took many forms, and over the course of war after war, our lands were taken from us. We were pushed as far west as the end of this fair land. Now, we stand with our backs to the sea. Where do we go from here? Will we have to cross the Main—the great wide ocean?"

When any awareness came back to me, those last words would echo in my mind: "Where do we go from here? Will we have to cross the Main?"

Will we? my fevered mind asked. *Is there any hope on the other side? Why does pain and woe, blood and war, and now this famine, always come from the east? Will the same things follow us if we do go west? It seems they have before. Are the People of Danu still beneath the ground in this fair land? If only they would arise and help us. Perhaps they want us to leave so they can reclaim what was originally theirs.*

A few times, my fever abated. Then I wished I had the strength to rise from this sickbed, go into the fields, and look for one of those lonely remaining oaks. Then, I would kneel between the massive roots and listen, hoping to hear from the spirits of Danu. Or had they gone into league with the fairies? Was it true what Bridget had said that the fairies had brought this curse upon us, the curse of the black potatoes?

But I was too weak to do more than check on Johneen and Morgan. I knew Thomas was doing his best to care for them, but he wasn't well, either.

Whenever the moaning of the winds abated, Thomas would make his way to the stream and bring us cold water. Once I felt a little better, I used it to clean us up as best as I could. We had no soap, of course.

One morning, I awoke to silence. The winds had stopped. I could hear myself breathing again. Thomas was snoring beside me, and Johneen's shallow breaths sounded labored. I crept toward him and laid my hand on his forehead. He was still feverish. Then I moved toward the cradle where Morgan lay.

There was no sound at all from him. My heart began to race, and I noticed the bluish tinge on his thin skin. As my hands trembled, I laid them on his chest. There was no movement, no breath, no heartbeat.

I began to wail.

"What is it?" Thomas roused himself with effort.

My tears were streaming, and I couldn't stop myself from screaming. "He's dead! My baby's dead!"

Thomas was at my side as quickly as he could move. He took me in his arms and began to rock me back and forth. "Now, now, Maggie. He's in the arms of Jesus. He's not hungry anymore, and he's not cold."

"I wish I could join him," I sobbed, burying my face in his chest.

We didn't move for a long time. I heard my husband's heart thumping and felt his chest breathing in and out. At last he spoke, "All we can do is wait upon God to take us, if He so chooses."

"What have we done to be treated like this? Why is God punishing us like this?"

"We don't know if this is God's fault, Maggie."

"One day, Moira told me Sean heard that the English say God is punishing us for being Catholic and poor. That this famine is all Providence."

Thomas jerked his arm suddenly, and I saw him raise his fist in the air. "No," he shouted. "This is not God's doing! Maybe nature sent the blight, but it's the English who are leaving us to starve. All they want is to move us off the land, the land that used to be our ancestors'. I will not let them kill me. Somehow, I'm going to survive."

His breathing was labored from this exertion, and I waited for him to begin to relax before I spoke. "If you are going to survive, then so am I, and Johneen, too. Somehow, we must."

"Morgan deserves a decent burial," he said at last. "I'm going to see the landlord about a coffin."

"Oh, do you think he will even care?"

"Perhaps not, but I have to try. I can make it to the manse today while the winds have stopped."

"No, Thomas, let me go. Maybe he will take pity on a woman. You must stay and take care of Johneen."

"Are you sure you're strong enough?"

"I have the strength of a mother now." I gritted my teeth. "A mother who has lost her child."

To make the long walk to the manse I gathered all the rags of clothes I had and wrapped them around me. Then, I gathered the body of poor Morgan in my arms and moved to the door. As soon as I stepped out, the cold took my breath away, but I moved out anyway. I learned that if I breathed through my nose, the cold didn't hit me as severely as gulping air through my mouth. Still, there were times when I had to mouth breathe, panting for air in my exertion.

When I staggered to the iron gate, I praised the Lord

that it was open. I walked up to the main door and pounded with my feet. I needed both hands to keep hold of Morgan's stiffening body.

After some time, a servant cracked the door open. "What do you want?" he demanded.

"Please, sir, have pity on a poor woman. My child has died. Please find me a coffin so he can have a proper burial. I don't want his little soul to lie in Purgatory, naked and alone."

A deep, rumbling voice came from behind the servant. "What is it now, Parsons? Another poor mother begging?"

"This one has a dead child in her arms, sir. She asks for a coffin."

"Bah! More Papist beliefs, saying they have to be buried in a coffin. There's not enough wood in all of Ireland to build coffins for all these dead."

"She isn't even asking for food, sir." The servant's voice seemed to crack, and I saw him glance at me with a hint of sympathy.

"Tell her to go to the workhouse. They have coffins there." The deep-voiced man stepped closer to the door, moving the servant aside. "Get out of my house. Let the dead bury their own dead, as Jesus said."

The door slammed in my face before I could speak again. I was trembling with fury and the cold. As I turned to go, I staggered and nearly fell. There was nothing else to do but return to our cottage.

I'm not sure how I made it, but I know I fell several times. Somehow, I managed to stagger to my feet each time until the last. My head was spinning, and I could no longer move at all. Then I felt arms lifting me.

"I see the answer was no," came my sweet husband's voice.

I opened my eyes and found I was lying just short of our cottage door. He carried me inside and tried to break my iron grip on Morgan's body. At last, I let go and sobbed. "He said Jesus wants the dead to bury their own dead."

"I don't believe our Lord meant it this way," said Thomas. "He loved the little children and said, 'Let them come to me.' And so He is taking Morgan from us to be with Him."

"But the coffin?" My lips could barely move.

"I'll wrap him up properly, Maggie. You just rest now. You've done all a mother can do."

"And it wasn't enough." Tears were sliding down my cheeks. Thomas wiped at them with a chill finger and said nothing.

Then he walked out the door. When he came back, his jacket was gone. All he had left to wear was a threadbare shirt.

* * *

Soon after this, the winds and snows returned. We didn't have any sunny days for what seemed like forever. Days began to blur together. I couldn't get myself to rise from the straw mattress. I knew there were fleas and lice crawling on me, but I had no strength to swat or scratch them. Then, one day—or night—Thomas came to me with a bit of soup in one of our crockery cups.

"Here, Maggie, sip this."

"Where did you get this?"

"From a man in a black coat and a broad-brimmed black hat. He said he was from the Society of Friends."

"A friend? Can there be any friends left? He wasn't one of those souperists like we saw last fall? The ones who want us to—"

My strength left me, and I couldn't talk anymore. He tipped the cup, and the warm liquid filled my mouth. I managed to gulp and swallow. After two or three more sips, I began to feel warmer.

"You mean the ones who told us we could have soup if we denounced the Pope and became Protestant?" said Thomas.

I nodded.

"He didn't say a word about religion, Maggie. Sean says these Friends are called Quakers by most people; it has something to do with how they worship."

"How does Sean know so many things?" I was able to think a little more clearly now.

"He has an ear for any little bit of gossip, I think." Thomas smiled. "Moira, too. Then she tells all she knows to Sean. I'm sad to say, though. Their youngest son Porick has died, as well."

"Johneen?" Panic seized me, and I tried to rise but had no strength to.

"He's fine, Maggie. Just relax. He had a full cup of soup, too."

I lay back and closed my eyes. My stomach began to gurgle. The soup was the first thing I remembered eating for such a long time. I hoped I wouldn't be sick. Then I must have fallen asleep, for the next time I opened my eyes, I felt warmer than I had in so long. There was a peat fire burning again. A brightness was shining in through the smoke-hole in the roof.

"Mama, it's spring," said a small voice.

"Is it?"

"Yes, Mama."

"Please come give me a hug and a kiss, son."

He gently kissed my cheek and cuddled next to me.

"I think we've made it through a long, cold winter, my child."

It wasn't until a day or two later that I noticed the cradle was gone. When I asked Thomas about it, he said, "I was able to pawn it. I have five pounds in a safe place." He refused to say more.

Many days passed before he told me the rest of his story. Johneen was slumbering on our old straw mattress, and Thomas sat on the edge of it near me.

"My older brother Patrick has left," he said.

"Left? This world?"

"Ah, no," he smiled. "Only our world—Ireland. In the winter of forty-four, he made it to Dublin and sailed in a packet boat to Liverpool. It took several weeks, he said, but at last he was able to get passage on a ship to Canada by working as a sailor. He replaced one who had died of the fever."

"How do you know all this, Thomas?"

"He sent me a letter from Montreal, Canada. It must have taken him a long time to get there, or perhaps the letter was delayed, as often happens, for it came to me just as this winter ended. You had been so sick that I waited until now to tell you. There is work for strong men, he says. And he's promised to send us some passage money once he has saved enough."

"This Canada must be a wondrous place if a man can earn money like that."

"Well, it hasn't happened yet, but we can hope."

Silence settled between us for several minutes. At last, I spoke. "There is no hope of staying here in Ireland, is there?"

"No, I don't think so. The English have pushed us further and further west, into the most infertile and desolate lands, even right up against the Atlantic coast."

"Our people, the Gaels, have always been pushed west, my granny used to say. Now that we've reached the ocean, we must cross it to the west. But perhaps there's hope on the other side."

He pulled me close and enfolded me in his long arms. "We must never give up hope, Maggie."

I wish Emilia would come explain more of this to me. But for some strange reason, she comes and goes. Perhaps there is only so much she can do. I don't understand what this time travel is all about.

CHAPTER 11
You Call These Works? Spring 1847

Near the center of the empty village market, we and our neighbors huddled as a man talked, almost shouting. I moved in closer, but still couldn't make out what he was saying. Ahead of me, Johneen sat on Thomas's shoulders. I felt a movement on my left and saw Moira step beside me.

"Can you hear what he's saying?" I asked.

"A bit," she said, "But my English isn't so good."

"Ah, no wonder I can't make anything out. All I know is Irish."

"I'm sure he knows that," she sighed. "He must think that the louder he shouts, we will understand English. I can make out some of it. He says the public works projects are being restarted now that the snows are gone. They pay only a pittance, my Sean says. He walked ten miles to a work site last time. Had to leave home before dawn to get there in time. The little coin helped us buy some oats. Prime Minister Old Lord John in London has lifted the price controls on grain, the merchants claim. It costs twice as much for a bag of oats as it did last year."

"Or the merchants are lining their pockets again, Moira."

"Besides, it's next to nothing Sean was paid. He had to work all day and then walk home in the dark. He came home so tired he collapsed on the bed without eating a bite of the small oatcakes I had to offer. I'd sold my last warm dress to buy the grain.'

The Englishman's speech ended, and Sean came over to us. I could see how gaunt he was. His ragged clothes hung on him like a scarecrow.

"Come, Moira," he said, his voice weak and hoarse. "It's just more of the same fake-work, make-work. Like last time when they had us shovel rocks and gravel from one pile to another. Once that was done, we were told to move it all back where it came from."

"Why would they do such a silly thing as that?" I asked.

He shrugged. "Some of the other men who had better English said the idea was to give a little money to us, but the work had to be nothing useful. Otherwise, it would interfere with something they kept calling 'economics.'"

"That's so ridiculous," said Moira.

"One fellow told me the English want 'natural process' to take care of itself. If we actually built a road, it would be helpful to someone, and that would interfere with their 'natural process.'"

I was shaking my head in confusion as Thomas came up, Johneen still on his shoulders. "Here," I said and reached up to help him down. "Don't wear your Da out."

Thomas couldn't hide his slight sigh of relief from me. Taking a deep breath, he spoke, "This time, I think I'll give this work project a try, Sean. They say we'll be building an actual road."

Sean shook his head. "It's not worth it to me this time. I spent all my energy for next to nothing. Why can't they give a man a good wage for a good day's work? I've heard some of the lads from across the way say that when their payday came, there was no money to be had. The paymaster shrugged and said it was still being collected in England."

Sean seemed to be babbling more than usual. Moira glanced at me, and I saw the concern in her eyes. Was Sean starved to the point that his sanity was teetering on the edge?

I'd heard Bridget talking of a new kind of fever that caused people to lose their wits. "Old Paddy told me about it last fall," she'd said. "Poor soul died in early winter. He said every time there is a famine, the fever follows. Kevin had to bury him in rags before the ground froze hard as a rock. There was no way to get a coffin."

I remembered looking into her bloodshot eyes on that icy winter day and wondering if she had this fever. *Poor Old Paddy,* I thought. *That was when I first learned he had died. At least Bridget isn't going on about fairies and banshees.*

As I remembered this conversation now, I shuddered. My granny had always said the cry of the banshee was the harbinger of death. *There's been too much death. When will it end?*

My husband's voice cut into these thoughts. "I have to try something, Sean. I promised Maggie we'd survive this, and I intend to keep that promise."

"Good luck with that." Sean rolled his eyes.

Moira had no glimmer of hope in her eyes either. "We're all going to die," she moaned. "There's no hope unless someone helps us."

As the conversation continued, Johneen moved to me, and I took his hand. Now, I felt his hand begin to tremble.

"I'm taking Johneen back to the cottage. You're frightening him." *And me,* I added to myself.

As I walked back, I tried to reach the girl in my mind. *Emilia, can you hear me? How can we survive this?"*

'I'm here to be sure you will.'

But what about all the others? Like Sean and Moira? Kevin and Bridget?

'I don't know for sure about them. Over a million Irish will die before this is over. But many more will live by leaving Ireland for England and the British colonies.'

Leave Ireland? Is that what we must do? But this is the only home I've ever known. All my ancestors are buried here, especially my dear old granny over in the churchyard.

'I know, Maggie. But if it's a choice between life and death—'

No! I won't leave here. Not yet. Just leave me alone.

She had heard, I suppose, for her voice didn't answer.

The night before he was to leave for the works, just before dawn, Thomas and I lay awake, trying to ignore our hunger pangs.

"Do you remember the good times, Maggie?" he muttered.

"They seem unreal now. Like a long-gone dream."

"That's how we met, remember? My father was playing his fiddle for a dance, and you came. I was smitten at the first sight of your auburn hair and shining dark eyes."

"You cut a handsome figure yourself, Thomas. It was your dancing that caught most of my attention, though."

"Ah, so that's why you came to join me in a jig."

"Of course. But the reels were the best, all of us winding in and out and all around."

He reached over and took my hand. I could feel his bones through thin skin.

"I wonder if days like that will ever come again," I sighed.

"Perhaps they will, Maggie."

We lay in silence then, listening to Johneen's soft breathing.

"I had to pawn my father's fiddle," whispered Thomas.

Tears sprung to my eyes. "Oh, you shouldn't have. It was the only thing he left you."

He gave a long sigh. "I know. But it would have done no good if we were all dead. Besides, he hadn't had the time to teach me to play it. His work was too hard in the later years. I think I have enough now for a ship's passage for the three of us."

A ship's passage. So that voice, Emilia, must be right. Our only hope is to leave this island—our home.

In the end, Sean decided to go with Thomas to the works project, after all. "They have eaten all their seed potatoes," my husband told me after the first week of work. "And I hate to admit it, but this road leads nowhere. As Sean said, we can't mess with the 'economics.'"

I didn't say anything about that, for I was just waiting for the coin to come so I could buy some grain. Our seed potatoes were getting low.

At least now, the days were getting longer as spring arrived. When their payday came at last, though, Thomas came home empty-handed.

"I'm sorry, Maggie. The paymaster just shook his head. He said it takes longer to get things here to County Kerry because we are so far from cities like Dublin, Galway, or Cork. There are no good harbors on our windy, rugged coast."

"See, we *do* need roads that lead somewhere," I moaned. "Why can't people see that?"

The next morning, Thomas was too weak to get out of bed. *What can I do now? There are only seed potatoes left. I have no money to buy oats.*

I sent Johneen to find some dandelion greens and perhaps a few wild onions. When he came back with them, I made a weak broth and took this to Thomas. It was better than nothing.

"Now I understand why people down Cork-way are

attacking the loads of grain bound for England," he sighed, once he had the strength to.

"But they will be sent to the lockups. Or worse, transported to the penal colonies."

"Aye, but they feed prisoners, Maggie."

"I'd sooner go to the workhouse than have you in jail," I said.

"No, not the workhouse. They separate the men from the women and the children from their parents. From what I've heard, it's a terrible place. There are no beds, just straw on the hard floors. The food is awful, and they work you hard for no pay. The idea is to make you never want to go there, to make you want to leave and get a job."

"But there are no jobs—except those awful 'works' of the English," I moaned.

My heart was sinking. Was there no hope anywhere? After I'd sat for a few moments in these thoughts, a knock came at the door. It was Bridget. Her eyes were shining brightly, and at first I was afraid she had the fever, but then she smiled.

"There's going to be a soup kitchen in the village," she said. "Anyone can come and get a ticket for free. Then they can have soup."

I looked toward the ceiling. Maybe there was some hope after all.

* * *

This soup shop was run by the Society of Friends, as they called themselves. And at this point, they seemed to be the only friends we Irish had. They didn't badger us about our faith or try to convert us to their religion. I was glad they were back, as I vaguely remembered the cup of soup Thomas had brought from these Quakers last winter. Besides the soup, they had some clothes to offer, even a blanket, and if we felt ill, they did their best to give us some doctoring.

They wore simple, dark clothing and didn't seem rich. One day, I heard one of them say to another, "We've been fortunate that our people in America have donated so much money and clothing to help these unfortunate people."

"The need is so great, though," the other replied. "I'm not sure it will be enough."

The nourishment from the soup, thin as it was much of the time, did revive us. Thomas was told he would be laid off from his work project by summer. The snows that had piled higher than we'd ever seen finally melted. Bits of green weeds and grass peeked out of the ground and grew quickly in the frequent rains as spring came and we approached planting season.

"I'm going to plant the last of our seed potatoes," Thomas announced one morning.

"There are so few," I moaned. "They will never be enough to get us through another winter."

He nodded and pulled me to him. "The best we can hope for is to have some new potatoes in late summer," he murmured. "Then we must set out for Cork before winter sets in."

"Cork? Why would we go there?"

"To take a ship to America or Canada. There's no hope in staying here. We'll just end up in mass graves."

"But I hear they have coffins at the workhouse."

"Oh, aye, there are coffins there," he said. "But they have hinges along the bottom edge. The body is tipped into a grave, and the coffins are used over and over again."

I gasped, and no words came to express my anger.

Thomas pulled me closer and kissed the top of my head. "We have to go while there's a chance for Johneen."

I nodded then. "Yes, a chance for him to live and have a future away from this God-forsaken place." Tears filled my eyes. "But it hurts to think of leaving everything we know to go to a strange, faraway place."

He hugged me tighter. I cringed when I felt the outline of his ribs poking through his thin skin. "It's a choice between death and life, Maggie."

I heard Emilia's words echo in my mind.

CHAPTER 12

The Housebreakers

After "Hungry July" passed that summer, we did manage to lift a few new potatoes. Some of them had black spots, but I cut them out and made a soup of what was left, which lasted us three days at one meal a day. There were only a dozen or so that seemed wholesome enough to bake in the fire. A couple of days after our soup was gone, I put three praties on the hearth to bake.

Johneen kept grabbing at them before they were done, burning his fingers in the process.

"No, son," I said. "We must wait for Da to get home from the works. We are blessed that he can still work. Then he can have supper with us. They aren't cooked enough yet, anyway. Come, let's go to the soup shop and see if they can spare us some."

The usual dinner time had passed, but the dear Quakers were still ladling out their warm soup. This time, there were pieces of celery and carrots floating in the broth. I blew on mine to cool it enough to eat, even as Johneen scalded his tongue because he was too hungry to wait.

As he fussed about it, I tried not to scold him, for I knew his hunger was driving him. *The poor lad,* I thought to myself. *I wonder if we will ever make it through this.* While these thoughts filled my mind, one of the Quaker women walked up to us in her plain, linen dress. Without a word, she handed each of us a piece of warm bread.

"Ah, bless you," I cried. "Doesn't it smell delicious, John?" In the presence of strangers, I didn't add the fond family ending of -een to his name.

He only nodded, for his mouth was stuffed with nearly half the piece.

"He's a fine young boy, ma'am," she said. She glanced around to be sure no one noticed as she handed my son a second piece.

"Why do you do this? If you weren't here, we'd have no hope at all."

"The Lord wants us to minister to His poor and needy, wherever they are," she said. "Thou art one of His children." She waved her arm, indicating all the people gathered around. "All these are His dear children. I only wish we could do more for Thee. There are so many more scattered in these hills and dales that we cannot reach them all."

"The English have no hearts," I blurted out. "They just want to see us gone."

"Thou must not blame all the English," she whispered, moving closer. "There are many who care, but they are not the ones in charge. There are people across the seas who care, as well. Some have sent us money so we can help as many as possible." She moved away from me. "I must take bread to others now," she said.

By this time, my son and I had drained our soup bowls dry, and the bread was all eaten, except for one I'd convinced him to save for his father. "Come now," I said. "We must get home before Da comes."

My legs shook when I rose. The scene around me whirled once or twice, and I nearly stumbled. "Ma, are you okay?"

I straightened up as best I could. "Yes, son. Not to worry. Just rose too fast from the ground."

As we walked back past the greening fields of the landlord's recently planted grain, I was tempted to trample some. His treatment of us was so inhumane. Beyond the grain fields were sheep grazing in a pasture encircled by dry-stone walls. The smell of them turned my stomach, not in nausea but in hunger. I grabbed Johneen's hand and pulled him along quickly.

When we reached the other side of the pasture, a man was eyeing us in suspicion. By his clothing, I knew he was one of the farmers who leased five or six acres from the Earl.

I nodded and tried to smile as we walked by. "Good day to you, sir."

He looked at us sharply but then nodded and responded. "Good day." Then he stepped closer, and my heart began to pound. "Don't be afraid," he said. "I know you are among the poorest of the Earl's tenants, but you are not the only ones in danger here."

"What do you mean?" I was so surprised that I forgot to address him properly.

He didn't seem to notice as he stepped even closer to talk in a low, quiet voice. "Our landlord, yours and mine, has gotten himself deep in debt. The English expect the landlords to pay for our feeding and upkeep until this famine subsides. Many of them, including our Earl, seek buyers for their estates, promising them completely open grazing land."

"With no tenants to deal with," I whispered as his words sunk in.

He nodded. "Not just you poor half-acre tenants. All of us."

"But you have a good farm here, grain, pigs—"

Just as I said that last word, I glanced toward where I heard some pigs squealing. To my horror, Johneen was kneeling beside the pig trough, pulling out bits of semi-edible food and gobbling them down.

"John!" I screamed and ran toward him. "How disgraceful!" I grabbed his arm and jerked him away from the trough. He just wiped his chin and looked at me. When I felt how frail he was and saw the deep hunger in his eyes, I began to cry. I turned to the farmer and moaned, "I'm so very sorry, sir." I couldn't raise my eyes to meet his face.

"He's not the first one I've seen over there," he said. "And what does it matter? The landlord is going to take it all from me anyway. Soon, the housebreakers will come, and we will all be put out."

"You mean—evictions? But we've nowhere else to go."

"He doesn't care. All he wants is to be rid of us so he can sell the land for grazing. That's what the English want—more cattle and fewer Irish."

"But it's our homeland." Tears were still streaming down my cheeks.

"As I said, even farmers like me are no longer wanted. Haven't you noticed how empty the clachan is? There are no stalls with shopkeepers. They've left, either because they have nothing left to sell or because no one can afford to buy what little they have."

"Is Ireland doomed then?"

"They've taken it from us, step-by-step, for centuries. Now, the end is coming. One hundred years ago, they did the Highland Clearances in Scotland. Nothing is left there but tumbled ruins of a few crofts and castles—and thousands of grazing sheep. It's been coming ever since Cromwell swept across this isle with his Ironsides Army two hundred years ago, raping and pillaging and then giving our land to his soldiers for their 'faithful' service."

"Whatever shall we do?"

"Pray our landlord doesn't wait until winter as some did further west. There, people were driven from their homes in a terrible storm on Christmas Eve."

"Holy Mary!" I blushed as this oath escaped my mouth.

"Some have found ways to salvage enough stone, timbers, and thatch to build little scalpeens in the ditches. But many are dying there from the cold, starvation, and disease."

Words forsook me in my horror.

"Ouch, you're hurting me, Mama," Johneen said just then.

I looked down and saw I was gripping his arm so tightly that his hand was turning blue. In shame, I released him. "I'm sorry, son."

"Some say emigration is our only choice. It's leave or die."

Loud grunts and squeals began coming from the pig trough. The farmer turned toward them. "Even they are fighting over getting enough food," he muttered. "Good day, ma'am."

As Johneen and I stumbled away, the farmer began beating the pigs back from the trough, so only two or three could eat at a time. My mind was numb as we made our way to our cottage. When it came into sight, my chest grew tight with fear. Could it really be true? Would housebreakers come soon and tumble down the only home our family had ever known? Would we also end up cowering in the ditches and eventually dying there?

* * *

Thomas did not arrive home until after dark. I'd let Johneen have one of the potatoes from the hearth but didn't eat one myself. Once he was asleep in the middle of our bed, I collapsed onto the one stool we had left. The other had been sold weeks ago to buy a little bag of oats.

When Thomas finally arrived, I could see how weary he was, with dark circles under his eyes and blotches of red beginning to appear on his skin. I hoped the look in his eyes wasn't feverish. I didn't say anything about my conversation with the farmer until he'd gobbled the Quakers' bread, and we'd eaten our potatoes.

"The farmer up the lane says the Earl wants to sell all his land for grazing. There will be no place for tenants then. We're all going to be evicted."

Thomas was silent for so long after I spoke that I wondered if he had heard me. "Ah, it was only a matter of time, Maggie," he said at last. "I've been hearing of it from many people at the works. Did you know that I passed three dead men lying beside the path on my way home? There are women and girls at the works now, too."

"What? How awful! The work must be very hard, from what I see on your face."

He held up scraped and chapped hands. "Ay, 'tis very hard. But they have no choice if their men are dead. Someone must earn some coin if they expect to eat."

Tears flooded my eyes, and I fell into his bony embrace. "What is the point if they're going to put us out with nowhere to go but the ditches?"

"More are going to the workhouses now, as terrible as they are. But those places are overcrowded, so fevers are running rampant."

"We mustn't go there," I sighed. "I guess you are right. Our only hope is to try and sail to America. "Is it a long walk to Cork? I've never been past the far side of the clachan."

"I'm sure it's a long walk. My walk to the works is getting close to ten miles now, but that's a small bit compared to the way to Cork. We'll have to sleep in the ditches along the way."

"What will we find to eat?"

"I really don't know, Maggie. Perhaps we will find more of the kind Quakers."

"And if we don't?"

"Then we will just keep trudging as long as we have breath left in us."

"Holy Mary, protect us," I murmured.

"Aye," he said. "We must remember to say the Rosary, 'Holy Mary, Mother of God, pray for us sinners, now and at the hour of our death'—"

"Amen," I sighed. He put his arms around me and pulled me close. "We must eat the rest of our new potatoes to build up our strength. I'll get up early to raise what I can and put some on the fire for breakfast. We have enough peat in here for the morning fire. You and Johneen must go to the soup shop at dinner. Then, when I get home, we will eat another potato for supper."

"At that rate, our potatoes will be gone in less than a week, Thomas."

"Aye, but why should we let the housebreakers have them?"

"Are you still going to the works? What if they come while you are away?"

"I'm going to finish out the week so I can get paid. That coin will hopefully buy us a bag of grain for the long walk. If we can build a small fire each night, we can at least have a little stirabout to warm our bellies before bed."

I closed my eyes, blinking back tears again. "We have to survive this somehow, Thomas."

He nodded, but he didn't say a word. His breathing was so shallow that I wondered if he had enough breath to speak.

* * *

Two days passed as I followed my husband's instructions. I began to feel much stronger with three meals a day, meager as they were. Some proper color began to come to Johneen's face. I didn't see quite as much health returning to Thomas, though. He had to work so hard, and his only meals were a potato for breakfast and one when he got home. We rarely spoke. There didn't seem to be much to say anymore. We knew doom was hanging over our heads and drawing closer with each passing day.

The third day he finally received his pay and went straight to the clachan to buy the oats. While he was gone, I stood in our doorway and listened to the cottages around us. There had been no sound from Kevin and Bridget's house for the past few days. Thomas told me Sean had not been to the works for a week because he had the fever. All I heard from their cottage was an occasional low moan.

When Thomas returned, he set a small bag of oats on the floor. "I'm sorry, this was all I could get. The prices keep rising. The housebreakers are working this way. They're just beyond the clachan."

The first we heard of them was the moans and screams coming from the path to the clachan. Then, we saw what appeared to be a whole troop of soldiers, followed by some Irishmen wielding crowbars, saws, and clubs. I grabbed Thomas's arm and hid my face in his shoulder.

"Quick, Maggie, grab the praties off the fire and wrap them in your dress."

In the meantime, he was stuffing the bag of oats into his shirt. He was so thin that it looked like nothing was hiding under there. I rested the praties where they looked like what used to be my bosom. I also tucked our small cooking pot below my waist, hoping I'd look with child, and no one would see the pot. Then I grabbed Johneen's hand and wrapped the blanket from the Quakers around him. It was getting a bit ragged by now. He had outgrown all his clothes over the past year, and they had turned to rags. At least the blanket covered them. I tried to tuck it around him, so it wouldn't fall off when he moved. Then I pulled down the old muslin curtain and wrapped it around my shoulders.

The next things we heard were shouts and chopping sounds. Looking across to Old Paddy's mud hut, we saw them smashing it in with their crowbars.

"Why are they doing that?" I asked. "No one lives there anymore."

"So we can't use it for shelter, I'm sure," Thomas said through gritted teeth.

Then they did the same to what was left of Moraigh and Artan's hut, which had been empty for over a year. When they came to Bridget and Kevin's cottage, someone opened the door and staggered back, gagging and holding his nose.

"There's only death in there," he muttered.

Two men placed themselves on either side of the cottage and climbed onto the roof. With a long saw, one man on each end, they cut into the beam which held up the roof. Then one tied a rope around the center of the beam. Both jumped off the roof and began to pull at the rope on the side of the cottage where the door was. Soon, the beam gave way, and the roof came crashing down into the center of the cottage. Another man stepped forward with a burning torch and lit the thatch on fire.

I buried my face in Thomas's chest, but I could still see the licking of the flames in my mind. For certain, Bridget and Kevin were dead, but I wept to think of their bodies being burned in their own home like pagans, with no proper Christian burial.

Soon, the housebreakers moved to Sean and Moira's cottage. It was smaller, and the mud walls were crumbling and thin. They began to hack away with their crowbars, and the walls tumbled inward.

Suddenly, a weak cry reached my ears, and I saw a stick-thin figure crawling out the door. Without thinking, I ran over and pulled the person toward me. "Siobhan," I said in surprise. "Is anyone else alive in there?"

"All the rest are dead," she sobbed, leaning on my shoulder. She was so thin I barely felt her weight at all.

"Come with me. You will be my daughter now."

The troops had been busy watching the walls of the hovel cave-in. "There's no one alive here, either," one of them called. So the man with the torch set the thatch ablaze.

Our little house was the only one standing now. A man with a badge on his coat walked up to Thomas and began the read something.

"What is he saying? My English is too poor to understand."

"I think it's a notice of eviction for non-payment of rent," muttered Thomas. "He's a sheriff."

By now the men with the saw were on the roof cutting into the center of the beam. Two others went inside and pushed at the gables where our roof support was anchored.

"Is this all your family?" the sheriff asked. "Is anyone dead in there?"

I grabbed Johneen's hand and put my arm around Siobhan's shoulder. "These are my only surviving children, sir."

"Do you have anything of value in the house?"

Thomas shook his head. "Everything has been sold to buy grain except the straw mattress we slept on. It's too filthy to keep."

The man stepped back. "All right, men. Bring her down."

Thomas and I moved away, trying not to look at our home being demolished. The men on the rope pulled, and soon, the beam gave way. It crashed into the middle of the cottage, its ends still clinging to the gables.

Some of them began to hack at the walls with the crowbars. "Never mind," called the sheriff. "Leave it. We have more houses to tumble before nightfall."

By this time, the four of us were crawling into a dry ditch. We huddled together and hoped the man and his troops would leave us alone. But he stalked over to where we sat and said, "If I were you, I'd get to the nearest workhouse. It's the only place you vermin belong."

I felt Thomas stir as if to rise to his challenge, but I gripped his arm, and he stayed beside me. "Maybe we can shelter under one of the gables of our wrecked house after they leave," he whispered in my ear.

But this was not to be, for the man with the torch tossed it into the pile of thatch that had fallen with the roof. As he stalked past us, he gave a wicked, toothless grin. "I earned my shilling today. If you were smart, man, you'd do the same. At least housebreakers get a bit of food for their labors. I have to survive somehow." His eyes looked sad. Perhaps he regretted what he was doing after all.

I could hear Thomas grinding his teeth as he muttered. "I will never profit from the pain of another."

'Desperate people are forced to desperate actions, Maggie.'

Emilia? What are we supposed to do now? We have nowhere to go.

'You will have to find shelter where you can. Many people hide in the ditches and try to put some sort of shelter above them.'

It was almost as though Thomas heard these words, for as soon as the men were out of sight, he dashed over to what was left of the house and pulled out pieces of thatch that weren't aflame yet. He pulled the door down before it caught fire and laid the thatch atop it. Then he dragged all this to where we huddled in a ditch just past our little circle of ruined cottages.

"Maggie, can you help me?" he wheezed. Just this small labor had taken his breath away.

I rose and took one side of the door. Johneen and Siobhan climbed out of the ditch and began picking up pieces of thatch that had fallen on the ground. Thomas and I managed to wedge the door edges into the sides of the ditch to make a kind of roof. I then helped the children spread the thatch on the ground so we would have a drier place to sit.

"Well, now we have a *scalpeen*," said Thomas. "This will shelter us for the night."

Autumn was approaching, and the days were getting shorter. Soon, the sun had disappeared behind a cloud in the west. Above us, a night wind began to blow, and we huddled together for warmth. "Here," I said, taking one of the potatoes out of the bosom of my ragged dress. "Siobhan, you and Johneen share this."

She grabbed it from my hand, and I saw her fingers were so thin they were like claws. Before I could say another word, she bit into the potato, and it was half gone in another bite. I pried it out of her hand. "Johneen needs some, too," I whispered.

A light that hadn't been there before appeared in her eyes. "I thank you, Maggie, for taking me in. I'm sorry. I haven't had anything to eat for days."

I pulled her into my embrace. "We will give you a fair share of all we have, Siobhan."

Tears began to form in the corners of her eyes, and she clung to me. No more words came from her, only soft sobs.

"I'm so sorry that all your family died," I whispered. "We lost baby Morgan last winter."

Her head nodded against my chest. "Porick died first. At least Da was able to bury him. But then all the rest of us had the dysentery, and one by one they died. I was lying there praying for death when I heard the noise of the houses being beaten down."

I felt her shuddering breath coming in gasps and was surprised she had said so much. "You are our child now, Siobhan. You have a family again."

She spoke no more and just kept her head leaning against me. I stroked her tangled dark hair. Soon, her breathing became even, and I could tell she had fallen into a deep sleep.

Johneen was cuddled beside her, fast asleep as well.

"What now?" I asked Thomas as a light rain began to fall. Our old door was a solid one and kept most of the wet out. He moved closer to my other side so as not to disturb the children.

"I don't think we can stay here long," he said. "The landlord will run us off. And I don't think any other cottiers are left nearby. Even if they were, they would have no food to share with us. We must make for the harbor at Cork while we still have the strength."

Now I knew why he had insisted we eat three meals a day the past week. "How far is it to Cork?"

"I'm not sure. It might be fifty miles. I can walk over ten miles a day."

"But the children and I can't."

"Oh, aye. If we make five or six, we will be doing well."

"So, if Cork is fifty miles, we have up to ten days' walk ahead of us. Maybe more. When our food runs out, so will our strength."

CHAPTER 13

The Long Walk

Early the next morning, we gathered all we could carry or stuff into our ragged clothes. We ate the last two potatoes for breakfast. Thomas carried the grain sack of oats concealed beneath his shirt.

"We don't want to tempt anyone to rob us," he said.

I stuffed the cooking pot beneath the dress the Quakers had given me. I also had a pair of shoes for my feet, thanks to them. Johneen was wearing their blanket like a cape, and I gave Siobhan the muslin curtain to cover herself. Her clothes were in rags, and she had no shoes.

Thomas started off at an easy pace, but we had to stop at least three times that day to rest and catch our breath. As the hours wore on, all I could focus on was putting one foot in front of the other. Johneen was soon fussing, and Thomas lifted him onto his shoulders. Siobhan silently trudged beside me all day.

All across the Earl's land, we saw tumbled cottages and mud huts. Even the sturdier houses of the farmers were in ruins.

"Your farmer was right, Maggie," said Thomas.

When we reached the next clachan, a few people were straggling along the path ahead of us. One young-looking man with red hair stopped when he saw us and awaited our approach.

I clung to Thomas's arm. "Do you think he will rob us?" I whispered.

My husband just shook his head. "I don't know."

When we reached him, the man smiled a toothless grin. "Be ye headed for Cork?"

We stopped. "Aye," said Thomas.

"May I join ye? Me name is Michael. The rest of my family is dead. Company on the road is safer."

"We are about to stop for the night," I murmured. "We only have a little grain."

His eyes opened wide. "Ah, I haven't eaten in two days."

To myself, I moaned at spreading our meager food thinner, but Thomas smiled. "Do you know of a good place 'round here for a scalpeen?"

"Aye, follow me," said Michael. "It's best to move away from the clachan, so fewer people will see us."

Soon, he had led us to a deep, dry ditch where a large overhanging prickly shrub provided a natural shelter. Thomas kindled a fire from what the children and I had gathered. Michael offered to fill my pot with water.

"I know a good little spring nearby," he said. "It's sent by one of the Danu."

I shifted and hesitated to give him my pot, fearing he'd take it and run. But he had mentioned the Danu, and his eyes looked honest, so I handed it to him. Soon he came back, and it was filled with clear, clean water.

"Thank you," I said as he handed it to me. "Do you need a drink?"

"I had one at the spring, ma'am."

"Please call me Maggie."

"Try it yourself, Maggie," he smiled. "It's very good."

I took a couple of sips of the cool, fresh water, and then I convinced Thomas and the children to drink some, too.

"Bless the Children of Danu," I said. "And thank you again, Michael."

By now, the flames were leaping steadily from the small fire. Thomas set the pot in the middle but kept the flames from being smothered. Soon, the water began to boil, and I tossed in handfuls of oats from the sack. The only thing I had to stir with was a stick.

Once the stirabout was cooked, I pulled it off the fire with the stick through the pot's handle. It had to cool a little before we could eat because we had no spoons and had to dip it with our fingers. I was glad to see that Michael took turns with each of us. He even took a little less.

After the stirabout was gone, we each found a spot to lie beneath the prickly shrub. Again, Johneen curled up beside Siobhan. I stayed close to Thomas, but Michael didn't seem to mind lying a little way off by himself. With some food in our bellies, we all slept well.

The next couple of days continued in the same way. Michael seemed to know the country well and always found us a good sheltered spot for the night. We were moving into late autumn now, and the nights were chilly. When Michael moved closer to us for warmth, I didn't mind. He was gaining my trust.

By the fifth night, we were down to the last of the oats.

"I'm sorry to have eaten your food," said Michael as we took the last bites.

"Not to worry," said Thomas. "You have helped us find safe places to sleep. You earned it."

"Well, I have tramped around a lot of this country," Michael said. "I like to move about and discover new places."

"How far do you think it is to Cork?" Thomas asked.

"I'd say about twenty miles or so from here."

"Well, we're a bit over halfway then," I said. "If only we could do your ten miles a day, my Thomas, we would be there in two days."

"We can't, though. I'm thinking we have four or five days yet."

I sighed. "And our food is gone now."

"We should rest while we can and get a good night's sleep," said Thomas.

After we each had found a spot and settled, I lay awake listening to the others breathing in sleep. But I couldn't sleep. My mind kept seeing images of our ruined house and of my dead Morgan's blue face. Tears filled my eyes and ran down my cheeks into my ears.

This is all too much to bear, I thought. *Holy Mary, please just take us peacefully.*

'It's okay, Maggie. You are going to make it.'

Emilia? Where have you been? Can you help us?

'I've been right here in your mind all along. I know what you feel and what you think. But I also know that someone is coming close to you on the footpath you followed today.'

Oh, no! Are they robbers?

'No. They are a couple of refugees like you. You should get up and meet them. They have a bag of oats with them.'

What? Am I supposed to rob them?

'Of course not. Just befriend them like Michael befriended you.'

And they will help us?

'I believe so. Stand up now so they can see you.'

Struggling in my weakness, I stood. Not far from me were

a young man and woman, walking slowly. Their clothes were in rags like ours.

"Hello," I said.

They looked startled. "Who's there?"

"My name is Maggie."

"My name is Padrig, and this is Kathleen," said the man. "Have you found a safe place to sleep?"

"Yes, this ditch is dry and sheltered from most of the wind. There is room for two more."

The couple moved toward me.

"Please step carefully," I said. "There are four people here already asleep."

"Thank you," said Padrig. "We come from Ballydehob and don't know this area."

They found spots to lie down just before they came to where Michael was sleeping. I lay back down next to Thomas. "I hope you sleep well," I whispered. *And I hope I've done the right thing.*

'Don't worry. You have,' said Emilia.

CHAPTER 14

From Silence to Chaos

Sure enough, the next morning, Padrig and Kathleen woke when I did.

"Thank you, again," he said.

"Hey, we're all in need, but I still believe in St. Brigid's hospitality. I'm sorry we have no food left to offer you."

"But we do," said Kathleen. To my great surprise, she pulled a small loaf of bread from inside her dress. "We were able to get this in the last village. Since you have shared your scalpeen with us, we must share this with you."

"Oh, my—" was all I could say.

By this time, Johneen was stirring and woke Siobhan. Michael sat up, rubbing his eyes. Thomas heard my voice and was up with a start.

"Are you all right, Maggie?"

"I've never been better, dear."

"How about if we all have this for a bit of breakfast?" said Padrig.

Everyone began staring at our newcomers. "We don't have to take your food," said Michael.

"But we choose to share it," Kathleen responded. "Besides, we have a sack of oats, as well."

Thomas was looking at me with questioning in his eyes.

"This is Padrig and Kathleen," I told everyone. "They happened by just before I fell asleep, asking if there was a place they could sleep. I invited them to join us since we had room."

"And more bodies means more heat on these cold nights," Padrig added. "If you will allow us to travel with you, we will share our food."

"Holy Mary and Brigid!" cried Michael. "Fortune has smiled on me again."

Without another word, Kathleen began to break pieces off the bread loaf and passed one to each of us.

"So now we are seven travelers," said Thomas. "That's a lucky number, I think."

"Sure, t'was luck that helped us find you," Padrig said.

"The scriptures say so," I nodded. Of course I wasn't about to tell any of them that it was the time traveler's voice in my mind that had told me about our new members.

"You must be heading for Cork, for there is no other good port in this corner of the country," Kathleen said as she finished chewing her piece of bread.

"Aye," said my husband. "We hear there are ships for America sailing from Cobh, Cork's seaport."

"It's our only hope, now that we've been evicted," I added.

"Same for us," said Padrig.

With a breakfast for a change, we set out and made good time that day. The land around us became more desolate as we moved through it. This was the southern edge of the Gougane Barra, Padrig told us.

"It's not good for growing much besides grass," he said.

"Well, that means the English will like it for their sheep," I sighed. "Along with all the good land they're taking from us."

"Now, Maggie," said Thomas. "Let's not throw a cloud on our hopeful day."

"I'm sorry."

We were past any land that Michael knew now, but this

time Padrig found a good sheltered spot for the night. Then he revealed the sack of oats he had been carrying. It was bigger than ours had been, and my mouth dropped open. *Emilia, you are a life-saver.*

'I keep telling you that's what I'm here for.'
I'm putting you right up with St. Brigid now.
'Well, thank you, but I'm not really a saint.'
So you say. But I say different.
There was no reply.

While Thomas and Michael built a cooking fire, Padrig took the pot I handed him and found a spring to fill it. Soon Kathleen was making stirabout. She even had a spoon to stir with.

We all slept better that night, knowing there would be food for a few more days.

Over the next couple of days, as we drew nearer to Cork, there was an eerie silence surrounding us. Not a single bird, not even a dog barking, could be heard.

"This whole area sounds like death itself," I murmured.

"Yes," said Padrig. "'Tis the silence of death you hear. This was a very hard-hit area. Everyone and everything here near Skibbereen is dead. The starving people ate anything left alive—birds, cats, dogs, rats—"

"Some, they say, even ate their own dead children," Kathleen whispered.

I could hear her as clear as a bell since the land was so silent. My skin crawled, and my chest ached as I thought of our dead babe, Morgan. I was glad Johneen was up ahead on Thomas's shoulders so he couldn't hear this.

"There are so few plants here, too," I said to change the subject.

"When nothing else was left, people tried to eat the grass, but people can't digest like cows. We only have one stomach," she added.

I shuddered again. "I remember the grass the children threw into our famine pot to try making it into food."

Silence fell on our group of seven. Johneen was leaning on Thomas's head now, fast asleep. I prayed he wasn't having hunger dreams.

At last, Padrig spoke again. "Before we found you folks, we saw some dreadful sights along the roads to the west."

He fell silent for several minutes before he spoke again in a low, mournful voice. "I hesitate even to tell, but since the youngling is asleep, I suppose I will. Once, I heard a mewling cry, like the cry of a kitten. But it was a babe off the side of the road, lying on its dead mother, trying to draw milk from her dried-up breast. He'd bit into it, trying to get some kind of nourishment." Tears formed in his eyes. "When I picked up the babe, he had gone limp. After only a few rattling breaths, he died. I had no strength or place to bury him, so I laid him back in his mother's arms."

I shuddered as I thought of the sight he described and shushed him so he wouldn't wake Johneen. For a long time, the only sound was our shuffling steps on the bare ground.

Then Padrig spoke again. "I know the things I saw will haunt my dreams."

"Me, as well," said Kathleen. "I think the worst were seeing the dead, staring into the cruel sky, their lips all dry and cracked and a trickle of green dripping from their mouths."

"Green?" I gasped.

"From the grass," she said. "Either they died trying to eat it, or it was pushed back out their throats as they died."

"They're all around us here—the dead. No one knows how many—buried in mass unmarked graves. This silence is their only dirge."

Looking around then, I expected to see ghosts rising out of the ground around us. My head began to spin, and I had to grab Thomas to keep from falling. The thought of sleeping near all those unmarked, hidden graves was almost more than I could bear.

* * *

After the ominous silence in the south of County Cork, the sounds of the city and its harbor were almost deafening. My first thought when I saw all the strange sights and smelled the overwhelming smells of massed humanity was: *Why am I doing this?*

I grabbed Thomas's arm and pulled him to a stop. "I want to go home," I murmured.

He drew me close to his bony side and put his arm around my shoulder. "We can't go back, Maggie. Only death awaits us there."

"But there are so many people, so much noise. I'm afraid."

Johneen drew closer and grabbed my hand. Even Siobhan had put a hand on my arm.

'This is the only way, Maggie,' came Emilia's voice in my mind. 'Thomas is right. If you go back, you will all die. Some will die crossing the Atlantic, but not all of you. There is a reason that the British ships are called Coffin Ships.'

Oh, if only I had died before all this happened. I could be buried in the churchyard next to my granny like my mother and father, and siblings are.

'That wasn't meant to be, you know. I'm sorry you must

go through this, but I'm told there is no other choice. Now there are some things I must tell you. Keep your cooking pot and try to buy some food to take on the ship with you, for the rations will be skimpy. If you could get an American ship, the accommodations would be much better, but all the American ships have sailed in the fall. Winter is just around the corner. Besides, their passage costs more.'

But how can we buy anything? We have no money except enough for our passage. Now we must pay for poor Siobhan, as well. The passage money that Thomas's brother promised hasn't come.

'You must pawn some more things, like your shoes. But keep the cooking pot. And be careful to check more than one pawnbroker to get the best price you can. Don't let anyone claim they can escort you to the finest lodgings where you can await your ship. The quays are full of runners and hucksters who are out to make quick money off the misfortunes of the poor. Siobhan will only need to pay half-fare, since she is under twelve. Because Johneen is so small, you may be able to claim he is a babe-in-arms, which means he will go for free. The first thing you must do is look the ships over and see which one seems most seaworthy.'

I have no idea how to look for that.

'Trust your husband and Michael. Just don't let the runners take them in. If you do need lodgings before your ship sails, go a street or two away from the docks.'

My mind is spinning with all this, Emilia.

'I'm sorry. I shouldn't have tried to tell you all this at once. Just tell Thomas to look the ships over.'

Okay.

Still leaning against my husband, I said in the most

confident voice I could muster, "We should look at the ships and see which one looks more seaworthy."

"Oh, aye," said Michael. "Let's walk along the quay."

As soon as we approached the harbor, men began swarming around us, taking our arms and pulling us toward them. I grabbed my own arm back and put both my hands around Thomas.

"Come with me," said two of them at once. "I can take you to the finest lodging."

"No," I snapped. "We are looking for a ship sailing today."

"Oh, no, you won't find one," said one of the hucksters. "You must look for lodging first."

"Let us be, so we can see for ourselves," said Thomas. I was so thankful for his strong voice and firm tone. The men backed off.

As we moved onto the docks, I glanced around. Johneen and Siobhan were still clinging to me. Michael followed close behind, but I didn't see Padrig and Kathleen. *I hope the runners haven't drawn them off.*

'They probably have,' said Emilia.

Oh dear, I wish I'd had time to warn them.

'I would if I could, but they wouldn't be able to hear me. All I can do is my best to help you.'

I gave a sigh. *So many helpless people. Why is this happening? Is there no charity left in this terrible world?*

By this time, we were walking past the three ships docked along the quay. The first had the name *Persephone* painted on her stern. It was only two-masted. The next one was named *Rachel Christine*, and then came *Anna Marie*. This last one rode higher in the water and had three tall masts.

"I like the looks of this one," said Michael.

"As do I," Thomas said. "I'm no sailor, but the timbers look strong and solid. She seems able to carry a good load."

Soon, a sailor came down the gangplank and began to walk by us.

"How do we get passage tickets?" Thomas asked him.

"Over yonder." He pointed to a booth back at the start of the dock. "Better hurry. She's nearly sold out."

We did hurry, but by the time we reached the booth, the man shook his head. "I'm sorry, but there are only two spots left, not five."

"But Siobhan and Johneen can sleep together, since he's so small," I said.

"That's still four bunks."

"Don't count me," said Michael.

"Still three. I can't do that either."

Thomas squeezed my arm when I took a breath to talk. "What about the *Rachel Christine*?" he asked.

"As it happens, she has four bunks left. Just enough for you. And she sails tomorrow afternoon with the tide. That will be sixteen pounds, four pounds per bunk."

Michael laid a five-pound note on the slab of wood in front of the man. "The fare is three pounds, ten shillings," he said, staring the ticket seller in the eyes. "You owe me a pound and ten shillings."

The man in the window rolled his eyes, but then shoved a one-pound note and ten shillings toward Michael, along with one ticket.

"Three bunks will be ten pounds and ten shillings for the rest of you lot," the ticket-seller snapped.

"But Siobhan is only eleven; that's half fare. And Johneen is merely three, a babe-in-arms."

"Aye, but the two of them will occupy a bunk, right?"

Thomas dug into his waistband and pulled out two five-pound notes.

"You still owe ten shillings," said the man.

I pulled the shoes the Quakers had given me from my feet. They had gotten worn down from our long walk. "Here, will these cover it?" I set them on the wood slab.

"How many miles have these old things walked?"

"At least fifty, sir, all the way from our clachan in County Kerry."

For an instant, his stare seemed to soften. "Oh, all right. They're probably worth ten shillings to someone. That will do." He handed three tickets to Thomas.

As we stepped away from the booth, a man carrying three straw-filled mattresses strode up to us. "You will thank me for selling you these," he said. "'Tisn't pleasant lying on bare wood all the way to America."

"How much for one?" Thomas said.

"Eight shillings and sixpence. But sir, you need all three, if not four, for your brood."

"I don't need one," said Michael.

"One is all I can afford," said Thomas as he handed the man the coins.

We should have talked to other vendors before we bought, I thought, remembering Emilia's words. *Ah, but it's too late now.*

"This is for you, Maggie," Thomas smiled. "I can't let my wife lie on a plank of wood all the way across the Main."

"Maybe the children should have it," I sighed.

"Well, we shall see when we are on the ship."

As we walked toward a line of shops across the street, I said, "Thomas, be sure to compare the prices these merchants are offering before we buy any food. Some will be overcharging to line their pockets."

"Aye, they're all probably doing that, seeing as we have no choice of another place to buy. But I'll do my best."

Once we'd found the shop with what we felt had the most reasonable prices for a sack of oats and a small bag of salt-dried fish, we had barely enough coin left to buy them. Michael even chipped in. And we still had to find lodging for the night.

What should we do, Emilia? I was starting to depend on this voice more and more, and with each word from her, I grew more grateful.

'Some ships will allow boarding twenty-four hours in advance, but if this one doesn't, you'll have to find reasonable lodging. Don't sleep out here in the open,' she warned. 'You'll be robbed for sure.'

We walked back to our new ship but were rebuffed. Since we'd first encountered the runners, Padrig and Kathleen had disappeared into the crowds. We hadn't seen anything of them. I hoped they were being treated well and not cheated, for they had been such a help to us.

Taking Emilia's earlier advice, I told my husband we should go a street or two away from the docks to find lodging. (I wasn't ready to tell him I was hearing a voice in my head.) At last, we saw a small inn with a sailing ship on her sign. "Perhaps that is a good place," I said and pointed to the sign.

We walked inside and found it dark and stuffy, but it wasn't cold and damp. *I hope this will be at least better for the children.* A man at the counter said, "I have only one room left, only two beds."

"That will do," Thomas nodded, "As long as Michael doesn't mind sleeping with me."

Michael gave a curt nod. "'T'will have to do."

"Seven shillings." The proprietor held out his hand. Thomas searched his pockets, but they were empty now. Michael's were, too.

I took the Quaker blanket from Johneen and held it up. "Will this be enough?"

"That's all ye have?"

"Yes, sir."

He hesitated for so long that I was afraid he would refuse us, but then his eyes looked into mine, and he nodded. As he took the blanket from my hand, I saw sympathy on his face. "It is a nicely woven piece of cloth," he said. Then he handed a key to Thomas. "Up the stairs and to your left."

We gathered what little we had left of our belongings and went to the room. There were straw-filled mattresses on the beds but no blankets. I curled up with Johneen and Siobhan and covered us with the old muslin sheet from our cottage. Thomas and Michael each lay close to the edges of their bed, on their backs, looking up at the ceiling.

I fell asleep almost at once, exhausted from the stress and noise of this day.

The next morning the innkeeper's wife set out some dark-colored bread and a pitcher of ale. That was all we had for breakfast, for we didn't want to waste our ship-food. The innkeeper's wife made sure we ate as much as we wanted. It appeared Emilia had led us to the right inn.

Shortly after we left the inn and made our way to the docks, we saw a line of people like us—all in rags—boarding the *Rachel Christine*. Johneen got excited and tried to run ahead, but Thomas grabbed him and swung him onto his shoulders. Siobhan clung to my hand.

"Well, now begins the next stage of our great adventure," I said, trying to sound optimistic.

No one made any comment.

We'll be all right now, I told myself as we got to the top of the gangplank and stepped onto the wooden deck of the ship. But in my heart, I knew the struggle was far from over.

We'd barely gone below and found our bunks among the hastily constructed wooden shapes in the dim light when the sailors were shouting through the hatch above us: "Everyone topside now!"

"Whatever for?" I asked Thomas.

Before he could answer, they called down again, "All on deck for rollcall! On the double! No exceptions!"

All the people began milling back toward the steps. Those who were able-bodied helped the old and weak ones climb the steep stairs. Children clambered or were carried in the arms of adults.

On the upper deck, the wind was brisk, and we huddled close together for warmth. The ship rocked and banged against the wharf as waves tried to push it toward the bay. A man with a long list of names began to call them out one by one. Each was answered with a "Here, sir!" He had to call several names twice because some voices were too weak to be heard above the banging of the ship, the slapping of the waves, and the murmuring of the crowd.

"Quiet!" shouted the man with the list. "The sooner this is over, the sooner you can go below."

In the meantime, we saw other sailors kicking at crates, pulling covers off lifeboats, and upending barrels. Not too far from Thomas and I, a groan escaped from one of the barrels. The sailor immediately tore the lid off and dragged a young man out.

"Thought you could stowaway, did you?" he sneered. He shoved the lad toward another sailor who took him by the scruff of his neck and hauled him down the gangplank to the dock.

The young man called out, "My ma has my ticket." But no one spoke up to confirm his claim.

"Your ma ain't here," called the man with the list. "Begone with ye!"

After what seemed like hours the rollcall was finished at last. Many of the older people shuffled toward the hatch and went down to get out of the wind. I started to move in that direction, holding Johneen's hand.

"No, Ma," he said. "I want to see the ship sail."

Thomas nodded. "Let him stay with me. This is the last we'll ever see of dear old Ireland."

At these words, I stopped and turned back toward the rail. The lines were being cast off. Sailors raised a small sail near the front of the boat, and as it caught the wind, the bow swung slowly away from the dock. As more sails were unfurled, the ship moved out into the bay of Cobh. Soon the tide was pulling us out toward the sea. Sailors raised the sails, and as the wind billowed them out, we moved farther and farther from the shore.

Tears filled my eyes. *It's just the wind*, I told myself. Though I knew better.

All too soon, the land began to recede from view and we couldn't make out many details any longer. The buildings became small smudges of color and the hills loomed grayish green in the background.

At last, I could no longer take the wind and my tears. A sharp pain filled my chest as I realized everything I knew in this world was fading from my life forever. I gave Siobhan and Thomas a hug and made my way slowly toward the hatch. Johneen was hoisted on his father's shoulders for a better view.

The deck was now heaving and slanting back and forth in the waves. Once, I nearly fell, but I reached the stairway at last and crept down. My eyes took a long time to adjust to the dimness, and I groped toward where I thought my bunk was. When I found it at last, I lay down and began to sob.

CHAPTER 15

The Crossing

None of us had ever been in a boat, and none of us had sailed on the mighty Atlantic. Just learning to walk on the heaving deck was frightening. I always kept Johneen close, gripping his hand. After a couple of days, however, he was steadier than the rest of us.

"Look at him," I said to Thomas. "I wish I had his sense of balance."

"It's because he's closer to the planking," my husband chuckled. "He's not as afraid of falling because he doesn't have as far to go."

The stench below was growing worse, so we spent as much time on deck as we could.

"Ah, to be young again," I sighed.

Just as I said this, the ship gave a sudden tilt to the right. I fell into the rail and found myself looking at the frothing waves. Thomas pulled me back, and I clung to him in fright. "Perhaps we should go below," I said.

"We must stay on deck as long as the weather permits, Maggie. We'll have too much time in that stinking hold when the storms come."

"How do you know that?"

"One of the other lads told me. He had a brother who sailed before him this past spring. This brother had earned enough at a job in America to send him passage money—in only a few months."

By now, the shifting of the deck had calmed. "Only a few months, Thomas? This America must be a wealthy place." I didn't say anything about his brother. *Has something gone wrong for Patrick? Is he even still alive?*

"Aye, that's what they say, my dear. I hope 'tis true. But first, we have to cross the wild Atlantic. We're late in the season and will have more storms, they say."

All of a sudden I was shivering, but I couldn't tell if it was from fright or the brisk wind in my face. Then, in a panic, I looked around for Johneen. He was standing beside the railing, and Siobhan was holding his hand. Thomas and I stepped over to join them.

"There's the last we'll ever see of Ireland," she said, pointing to a grey smudge on the horizon. "One of the sailors told me it's Mizen Head. The Blasket Islands are to the northwest, but they're shrouded in fog, as usual, and too far away to see, he told me."

As we'd sailed out of Cobh, Cork City's harbor, we'd watched every bit of our green island that we could see. Now, it had faded to a blurry gray, and tears began to fill my eyes. Looking at Siobhan, I saw her tears, too. I didn't look up at Thomas, not wanting to embarrass him. He put his arm around my shoulder. All four of us stood there until the last of the land faded from view.

That was the last we saw of any land for six long weeks. The seas grew rougher with each day, but we came on deck whenever the hatch to our mid-deck sleeping area was open. This ship had only two decks—the one exposed to the air and the one below where the cargo was carried. This ship's cargo, we were told, was pig iron, destined to be used for building tall buildings and bridges once it was remelted and shaped into steel beams and girders.

Where we slept was a makeshift deck of wood between the true decks. Carpenters in Cork had thrown up planks of wood across the belly of the ship and nailed up the bunks we were to live and sleep in. Each of us, we were told, was allotted ten square feet of space for us and all our belongings. The bunks were rickety, and so narrow that a man had to lie on his side. They weren't wide enough for anyone but a child to sleep on his back. Besides that, Johneen and Siobhan had to share a bunk, since they'd been charged only half-fare.

Thomas insisted that I use the single straw-filled mattress we'd bought. It was almost too wide for the narrow bunk, and sometimes, when the ship rolled and shifted in the waves, I rolled onto the floor. As the voyage progressed, those boards accumulated much filth and were often wet because waves splashed down the open hatch. It made me shudder to think that we had to walk in that muck with our bare feet, but there was no way around it.

During the first few days of the voyage, we were allowed on deck each morning to cook our food. There was a large metal wood stove where we lined up to take turns at one of the five burners. I was so thankful that we still had our trusty cooking pot. Each morning, we were given our allotment of the ship's rations. I heard people around me calling this the "Parliamentary Diet."

"Parliamentary?" I asked a woman beside me.

"Aye, the generous rich in London let us have a pittance of oats, biscuits hard enough to break your teeth, and tea. Sometimes a bit of sugar or molasses."

"No potatoes?"

"Of course not," she snapped. "All the potatoes have died along with thousands of paupers. Many of those on this ship were evicted by their landlords and given passage just to get rid of them. It was cheaper than paying for us to be in the workhouses."

"We were evicted, too," I said. "But our landlord gave us nothing for passage."

"Ah, one of the bad ones."

All I could do was nod.

Some days, the lines for the cookstove were so long that I never made it up to the front and had to carry my uncooked oats back to our tiny quarters. Those nights we gnawed on the biscuits slowly until they were finally softened enough to be chewed. Our allotment of water each day was one gallon per person. It was to be used for all our needs, whether cooking or washing. Most of the time, the washing didn't happen. This was when I began to notice the lice and fleas.

Somewhere in the second week of our voyage, a great storm rose. Waves rose high above the siderails and crashed onto the deck.

"Everyone below," the sailors called.

When the last person was down, they battened down the hatch and left us trapped inside the stinking hold. As the storm roared for several days, we had no way to cook food, but many of us were seasick anyway. There were buckets that people vomited in, but soon they were full. We were cut off from the two water closets in the bow of the ship. Many of us women had already been finding dark corners in the hold to relieve ourselves because the water closets were in full view of the sailors as they worked in the rigging. They enjoyed the show which was so embarrassing for us.

With the violent tossing and shifting of the ship, some of the pig iron cargo below us came loose and tossed its weight back and forth. This made the tilting of our between-deck world shift wildly. A couple of children were crushed as boxes of belongings were tossed about like toys. Then, bunks began to collapse toward the edges of the flimsy deck. The people in those bunks were forced to sleep on the filthy floor, for none of the crew came to repair them.

I kept hoping I would become accustomed to the stench, but it built up with each passing day. At last, after many dark and frightening days, the hatch above us was opened, and a crush of people surged toward the ladder that led to the deck.

Thomas held me back. "We'll get there in due time, Maggie. We mustn't get trampled for just a bit of sun." He handed me the cooking pot and a small handful of oats. "Perhaps they will light the stove."

However, many things were soaked with seawater, and there was no dry wood that day. I wasn't sure my stomach was ready for food yet, anyway. I just breathed in the salty air and tried to revive that way.

Some of the sailors had caught seawater in extra sails and were pouring it into tubs. A few women were washing clothes in the salt water, even though they had no soap. I would have done the same, but all I had left were the rags that barely covered my body. I would have had to stand about naked while I washed and hung them up to dry. I did manage to wash the old muslin sheet that Johneen and Siobhan had been lying on. It was full of urine and feces, for during the storm, they had been unable to even get out of their bunk to relieve themselves.

After that first storm, we had only three or four days of reprieve before the next one roared upon us. Once again, we were trapped in the hold. No water or food was sent down.

"I swear these sailors would treat a cargo of cattle better than they're treating us," said Michael.

A man in the next bunk raised his head. "I've heard they even treat slaves better."

"Well, of course," said the man in the bunk above him. "Slaves are property. They're worth money. We're just excess trash they want to be rid of."

* * *

It was about this time that some of the passengers in bunks around us began to show signs of ship fever. Their faces flushed, and they tossed and turned in pain. Some began to beg for water. Others rambled on in nonsense words, delirious. Soon I was too weak to get out of my bunk. I ached all over, especially my head. Time seemed to stand still as I lay in pain, flushed with fever. Sometimes, I sensed Thomas stroking my head with a small damp rag. I wanted to ask where he'd gotten the water but had no strength to speak.

After a long time—I have no idea how long—I began to feel a bit better. The throbbing in my joints and head began to abate. Darkness was all around me, and I hoped it was night. Or was I dead?

Then, I heard Thomas's voice as from a great distance: "Maggie, my darling?"

I managed to flutter my eyelids open. "Thomas?"

"Ah, praise Jesus, Mary and Bride," he moaned. "I thought I was losing you."

"Are you ill, too?" My voice was so raspy.

"Only a bit, my heart. Not like you and Siobhan."

"Johneen?"

"He's doing all right."

I sighed and closed my eyes again. It was too much work to keep them open any longer.

The next time I managed to open my eyes, daylight was filtering down from the open hatch. My head felt more normal, so I tried to slide out of the bunk. When I set my legs down, they collapsed beneath me.

In an instant, Thomas was at my side, helping me up. "There now, don't overdo it," he said. "You are still weak. There is a warming sun on the deck, though. Can you see it?"

I looked up, and sure enough, I could see a patch of blue sky through the hatchway. "Yes, I see it."

'Don't try to do too much too soon,' came that voice in my head.

Emilia? Are you still with me?

'Of course.'

Did you suffer as much as I did with this fever?

'I feel what you feel, Maggie.'

I'm so sorry.

'It's not your fault. Ship fever is part of the consequence of the filth you are being forced to travel in. Its true name is typhus fever, and it is carried from one person to another by lice.'

And we are surrounded by lice in this miserable hold.

'People don't know about the need for sanitation at this time you live. They don't know about germs and bacteria.'

What are those?

'Tiny organisms that cause disease. Much smaller even than the lice that carry them.'

But what can we do? They never give us enough water to drink, let alone wash ourselves. We're being treated worse than they treat cattle.

'Even worse than slaves are treated, for they have monetary value. But there is one thing you can do. Next time it rains gather as much of the rainwater as you can. Find an old piece of sailcloth or a pail to gather it in. Use that to wash yourself and your clothes.'

I have only one small pot. And our old muslin is too full of holes to hold water.

'Then, just stand out in the rain, even if it's cold. Let it wash over you. Pull the rags away from your body as much as you can.'

You want me to stand naked in front of those gawking sailors?

'It's the best I can do for you, Maggie. I'm sorry.' Her voice was almost a sob.

No, I'm sorry, Emilia. It's not your fault. It's the terrible English with their pride. They despise us and treat us like dirt.

'Unfortunately, many other people in the world are treated like this, as well.'

Suddenly, my thoughts and Emilia's words in my head were interrupted by a scream from the bunk across from me. I saw Siobhan thrashing and clutching at her arms and legs.

I tried to move toward her but was too weak. Thomas reached her first. As he tried to calm her, I noticed the red rashy spots across her body.

"She has the ship fever, too," my husband muttered. "Only much worse than you. She was starved much longer than we were, and her body is too weak to fight it off."

"Is there any hope for her?"

"All we can do is pray, Maggie."

We prayed and recited the Rosary through the next night. At last, her gaunt body stopped tossing and turning, and she lay still. When the light finally peeked into our dank hold between the ship's decks, I looked closely at her chest. There was no rise and fall of breath.

"Thomas," I moaned. "I think she's dead."

He held his hand close to her nostrils, trying to detect any breath. But he shook his head. "She's not breathing."

"No!" I cried. "I didn't take her in only to kill her in this hell hole." Tears blurred my vision.

"It's not your fault, Maggie."

I staggered toward him and clung to his shoulders. He tried to wipe my tears but to no avail.

"We must get some of the sailors to haul her up for burial."

"Burial? What do you mean? There's no priest, no ground for a grave. Only this wretched endless ocean."

"Aye. But she won't be the only one buried at sea on this voyage. Several others have been already. More than I can count. I hear the sailors say that sometimes a quarter of the passengers on earlier voyages have died."

All I could do was lean all my weight onto him and weep.

After Thomas settled me back in my bunk, I asked the question I barely dared to. "Where is Johneen?"

"He's lying safely above you on my bunk," he murmured. "Don't fear for him. "Now, rest. I must go tell the sailors."

I'm ashamed to say I was too groggy to ask about Michael. There was only silence in the bunks across from me where he and Siobhan lay. I must have fallen into a stupor of sleep because the next thing I knew, two men were hauling Siobhan's body up the steps through the hatch.

"Please," I called. "Let me come watch her."

Thomas came to my side at once and helped me up. As I rose, I saw he was holding a sleepy Johneen. I wanted to ask Thomas if it was safe to take him up, but there was no time. He pulled me up the steps behind the two sailors.

On deck, there was an old sail spread out, which they laid poor Siobhan across. Then they pulled it inward until she was tightly wrapped in it. From somewhere, one of them produced two heavy weights, which were placed by her feet. Then the sailcloth was pulled closed, and they began to stitch it together with quick, deft stabs of a needle and coarse thread. The last thing I saw was her emaciated face.

"Oh, my poor girl," I sobbed. "I so wanted to save you. And now all you get is a watery grave. No final rites to send you to the Father's arms—"

My voice broke into a wail. Strange words and sounds came from my mouth that even I didn't understand. I'd heard the village women keening at my family's funerals when I was a girl. Now, that long unspoken grief must have been what came pouring out of my broken heart.

By this time, they had laid the wrapped body on a plank of wood and heaved it up to the deck's rail. Two men stood at one end of the board and shoved it across the railing until it began to tip towards the heaving waters below. Then they pulled it back sharply. I covered Johneen's eyes with a hand as the body slid down the slanted board and dropped into the waves. In an inkling, it was gone.

My sobbing wails faded as my voice failed me.

* * *

No one had seen him come through the hatch, but we heard a garbled noise. When I turned, I saw Michael walking toward us, foaming at the mouth.

"He's insane with the ship fever," one of the sailors muttered.

At first, Michael lurched toward me, but Thomas shoved him back. "Stop, man! You don't know what you're doing. Go back to your bunk."

Michael raised a fist and tried to punch Thomas, but he lost his balance and fell onto the deck, still babbling incoherently. Then we heard a few words, "Arise ye dead of Skibbereen… come back from the deep…arise ye dead…"

He pulled himself up with the ship's rail and leaned over the water. "How can she rise if she's buried at sea?" he shouted. Before anyone could stop him, he flung himself over the rail.

"Man overboard!" cried a sailor.

But a stiff wind was pushing the ship away from Michael. His head disappeared in a wave. I never saw it again.

My weeping and keening resumed, and I leaned on Thomas's chest. He put his hand on my head and brushed my tangled hair back and forth. "He didn't know what he was doing," he said.

"How can any of us survive on this wretched ship?" I moaned.

"Come with me, Maggie," he murmured in my ear. "The waves are building, and the wind is rising."

Still carrying Johneen, Thomas pulled me to the steps leading down to our makeshift deck. Darkness closed in when the sailors battened down the hatch, as they always did during storms. We would be rolled and buffeted in darkness until this storm was over. We would have no food or water sent down to us. *How many days will we be stuck in this prison? Can I endure even one more?*

I didn't dare say anything to Thomas lest he think I was

going crazy with the fever, too. Instead, I crawled into my filthy bunk and lay on my side. I saw him move Johneen from the upper bunk to the one across from me, the one my little boy had shared with Siobhan, the girl who was gone. Above him was the empty bunk Michael had so recently left.

Darkness closed in, around me and in my mind. Funerals of all my family flashed through my head—my parents, my brothers, my sister. I was the only survivor now. They had died in a lesser famine in the 1830s. Thomas never mentioned if he had any surviving family besides Patrick. Perhaps his memories were as painful as mine.

CHAPTER 16

The Terrible River

I had no idea if it was day or night. Sometimes, the raging storm would toss me out of the bunk to a filthy floor awash with water and sludge. I didn't want to think about what was in it. Then, at last, the hatch was opened, and light flooded back into our prison-like world.

As we stumbled up toward the upper deck, a voice was calling, "Land ho!"

All who had emerged rushed to the rail and gazed in the direction the sailor in the rigging was pointing. There was a grayish-blue smudge on the horizon.

"Is it truly land, Thomas?"

"I don't see what else it can be." He put his arm across my shoulders.

"What is it?" a man asked beside me.

"We're nearing the Gulf of St. Lawrence," said another. "It's one of the headlands to the north, part of the island of Newfoundland."

I stood and stared at the blurry shape until my eyes began to burn. Then I laid my head on Thomas's shoulder.

"It looks like we've made it across the treacherous Atlantic," he said.

Sunlight beamed down on us from a break in the clouds, but it was a chill winter sun, and it was already sinking toward the western horizon.

"Everyone back below," bellowed a voice. "Trim the sails for the night."

"Aye, sir," said several voices.

I wish they would continue to sail at night, I thought. *This voyage wouldn't have taken as long. Perhaps more of us, even poor Siobhan, would have survived.*

'The American ships do sail at night,' came Emilia's voice. 'They have sturdier decks that can be cleaned more often, too.'

Oh, why did we have to end up on this ship?

'Don't be too downhearted, Maggie. The American ports limit the number of ships that can land. Canada is required to let all British ships land because they are part of the British Empire.'

But so many have died on this God-forsaken vessel.

'Still, you and your family are alive. You each have survived the typhus. The quarantine station will let you pass.'

Quarantine station?

'Yes. Any person who is ill must stay on Grosse Isle, an island up ahead in the St. Lawrence River, until they are well.'

Or until they die?

'Yes, and many do die and are buried here. In my time, there is a memorial to all the immigrants who made it across the ocean only to die in Canada. It is written in English, French, and Irish.'

I will have to learn either English or French, won't I?

'Yes. First, you will be in Quebec, where French is spoken. If you move further west into Ontario, the language is English.'

I shuddered, both from the cold wind and my fear of the unknown ahead of us. Emilia must have sensed my fear, for she added: 'Take one step, one day at a time, Maggie. I'm still here to help you in any way I can.'

After the long winter night in our bunks, dawn broke, and the sun's weak rays on the river revealed distant land on both sides of the ship. The water frothed with pieces of straw, cloth, and filth. Just as I wondered what could be the cause, sailors began to shout: "Down ye go. Get all your bedding and filthy stuff and throw it overboard."

Throw it overboard? All we'll have left is the rags on our bodies.

"Inspection boat is coming soon. Everything has to go," the shouts continued.

"Stay here with Johneen," said Thomas. "Hold tightly to his hand so he doesn't get lost in the shoving. I'll take care of our bedding. It's useless here in the Canadian winter anyway."

"Save our little cooking pot if you can," I called. "And any rations we have left."

"Any food left is spoiled and full of maggots," he called back as he moved to the hatch opening.

As soon as the remaining passengers had thrown their filth overboard, sailors began hosing down everything in what had been our mid-deck home for these long weeks.

How long has it been? I wondered.

'Most British ships take forty or fifty days,' came Emilia's reply. 'But some even longer if the weather turns foul. Your voyage was six weeks, forty-two days, which isn't bad.'

Still keeping a firm grip on Johneen, I looked at the mess floating away from our ship and wondered how many other ships had docked upriver.

Before long, a small boat came alongside our ship. A man jumped across the narrow gap and gripped a rope ladder, which he climbed to the deck. He paid no heed to any of us but went straight to the open hatch. He placed a handkerchief over his nose and mouth and descended the first two steps.

When he emerged only a few minutes later, I heard him say, "You're clean."

But I knew he was telling a lie. Even he couldn't stand the smell down there, the stench that all the hosings in the world could not erase.

* * *

As we stood on deck gazing at the bay, we saw it begin to taper as we neared the mouth of the St. Lawrence River. Just as Emilia had said, there was a long, narrow island reaching up into the river. When we got closer, we could see rows of white tents and a couple of hastily constructed wooden structures.

"Welcome to Grosse Isle," one of the sailors said with a laugh. "Just hope and pray this won't be your new home—or your final resting place."

Chills ran through my body at his words. Slowly, the ship plowed through the littered waters and came to a pier on one side of the island. There were three other boats there, already moored.

"Ah, we're lucky," the sailor laughed again. "We won't have to sit out in the gulf until there's a place for us."

Time seemed to crawl as our ship crept toward the pier. My hand gripped Thomas's so fiercely that he had to push it away. "Have hope, Maggie," he whispered. "And a few Hail Mary's won't hurt, either."

Without even thinking about it, the words began to run in my mind, "Hail Mary, full of grace, the Lord is with thee…"

Some men on the shore jumped onto the pier and grabbed the ropes our sailors tossed to them. After much calling, tugging, and cursing, we were secured to the pier at last.

"What comes next?" I murmured.

Thomas only shrugged.

After several more minutes, the ship's first mate climbed up to the raised rear deck. "The health inspector is occupied with one of the other ships. They say he will get to us tomorrow morning. Find a place to sit or lie down for the night."

"Where are we supposed to go?" someone shouted. "You've taken away our beds and the whole space between the decks is soaking wet."

"That's not my problem," the mate replied. "Find a spot somewhere, or just sit by the deck rails."

"Once again, they treat us worse than cattle," someone beside me sighed.

Thomas muttered, "Come with me Maggie." He scooped Johneen onto his shoulders and pushed his way through the crowd around us to one of the deck's rails. Using his size as best as he could, he parted the others, standing there until we had enough room for the two of us to be seated, our backs to the rail. He laid Johneen across our laps.

"I'm cold, Da," he whimpered.

I laid my arms across my son's small form, pulling as much of my rags as I could away from my body, and covered him. The winter winds picked up just then, and my teeth began to chatter. Thomas pulled me closer to him, using his arm to shelter me as much as he could.

Darkness quickly settled in the short winter days, and we held each other and tried not to shiver. Then a woman seated next to me murmured in my ear, "I hear tell the shivering is the way your body tries to keep warm. Don't try to stop it."

All I could do was nod. With the chattering of my teeth, there was no hope of speaking. Somehow, we made it through that long night. Just as the sun peeped over the horizon in the east, the mate called out, "Everyone line up for your health inspection."

We managed to stand, though my head was spinning from weakness. There had been no food rations doled out yesterday. In the crew's minds, our voyage was over, even though we were still trapped on their ship. A ragged line of emaciated people stretched in front of us as we started down the gangplank. Some were barely clothed in their rags.

As we got nearer, I could see a man in a long white coat looking at people's tongues as they stuck them out for him. Behind him was a red-capped nurse who put her hand on each one's forehead to see if they were feverish. She told her findings to another white-coated man, who sent some people to his right and some to his left.

There were still more than twenty people ahead of us when I began to hear women wailing and crying:

"No, that's my husband! Don't separate us!"

"My little girl! Please let her stay with me!"

Another woman tried to grab a child from the line on the doctor's left. A nurse stopped her. "She's sick, and you're not. She must go to the quarantine area."

"Oh, please let me go with her."

The nurse continued to hold her back. "You can't. There aren't enough beds as it is."

The mother continued to wail and tried to claw her way free, but she was too weak. At last, another passenger pulled her away and moved her into the line to the right. But her cries and wails continued to echo around us.

My heart was pounding by this time. *What if they try to take Johneen away? Or Thomas? And where is Michael? Why, I haven't seen him for—oh dear, now I remember. He jumped into the sea, crazed with the fever. Emilia? Are you still here?*

'Yes, I'm here,' came the comforting voice in my mind. 'I wish there was something I could do to help. If people are sick, they are sent to the quarantine tents.'

Those flimsy-looking white things?

'Yes. The men, women, and children are all separated. The only way a family can stay together is if all are healthy.'

How can these people be so cruel?

'They really are trying their best, Maggie. No one expected so many sick immigrants to arrive here—or so many ships. Four hundred and forty-one British ships will have docked here just in this one year, 1847, and over ninety thousand people will come through Grosse Isle. This is the worst epidemic year for typhus, what you call ship fever. Many people will die, even many of the doctors and nurses, too.'

It's those awful English in Parliament, isn't it? They have always wanted Ireland for themselves, and now they have their chance to be rid of us.

'Yes, some think that. Others don't know what's really going on. And some are trying to send money and food to help, but it's not enough. Too little and too late.'

By this time, I was trembling. I clung to Thomas's hand while he held Johneen close to his chest. *Oh, Lord and Holy Mary, please have mercy.*

We stepped up to the doctor and stuck out our tongues. He nodded. The nurse felt our foreheads and nodded to the man behind her. *Is this good or bad? Oh, please, let it be good.*

I nearly fainted with relief when the man nodded the three of us toward his right. We had survived the inspection. After going only ten more steps, I fell to the ground. Tears streamed from my eyes and I bowed low and kissed the cold, hard soil.

Thomas knelt beside me. "It's all right now, Maggie. We're in Canada."

"I'll never set foot on a ship again," I moaned.

"Aye," he whispered in my ear. "But we're on an island. There will have to be some kind of boat to take us upriver to Quebec City or Montreal, they say."

"Will they give us any food? Or clothes?"

"Come with me. Here, I'll help you to stand."

He lifted my body while still holding our little son. We both were little more than bags of frail bones. I was surprised that Thomas had any strength left himself. It must have been the love of God that gave it to him.

But then we were told to wait. The doctor stepped to the mate's side and talked softly to him. Thomas handed Johneen to me and moved closer so he could hear them. He was frowning when he returned to my side.

"That single man holds all our fates in his hands," he whispered.

"What did you hear?"

"If too many are sick, he'll quarantine the whole ship. See that ship behind us? It's under quarantine. No one can get off until more are well—or die."

My heart began to pound at the thought of being on that freezing deck for even one more night.

"Don't panic." Thomas patted my arm. "The mate told him our numbers. Three-hundred-fifty originally set sail, plus the crew. Ninety-five were buried at sea."

I shuddered as I remembered the splash of Siobhan's body.

"It's going to be okay, Maggie. He told the mate enough of us are well now. They won't hold back the whole ship."

Relief washed over me like a warm flow of wind.

* * *

Following the line of people, we found a tent where soup was being ladled into bowls. At the first sip, my stomach began to cramp. It was not used to such healthy food. I ate slowly. After we had eaten, we were sent to the next tent, where clothes of all sizes were laid out on tables made of slabs of wood laid across wooden props. I heard someone call them "sawhorses." At this word, Johneen laughed, a sound I hadn't heard for many months. "Look at the funny horses, Ma. They have four legs but no heads."

The sound of his tiny voice speaking again lifted my spirits. *What wonders a little real food and caring people can make.* Most of the people spoke French, and I understood nothing. But they used gestures to help us find suitable clothes, warm jackets, and even socks and shoes. *I think I've died and gone to heaven—except there are no golden streets, just this rugged, frozen earth.*

After this, we were directed to small boats, some with sails, but most with only oars. There were strong men at those oars, though. We were settled on benches and covered with blankets to protect us from the wintery winds as our boat moved up the St. Lawrence River.

I must have fallen into a deep sleep, for the next thing I knew, it was dark. In the distance, voices were shouting. Then lights appeared as we drew nearer. Hills rose above us, crowned with tall buildings, some shimmering with a few lanterns. We drew up to the docks that rose slowly up and down in the river's flow.

When we were told to leave our boat, we also had to leave the blankets, but at least we now had warm clothes. A few yards back from the dock stretched a long wooden building. People ahead of us shuffled through the door, so we followed. There were no beds inside, just straw-covered wooden floors. But they were steady, not heaving in the waves of the sea. I collapsed into the hay and fell asleep.

CHAPTER 17

A Miracle

The Canadian winter was long and snowy, chilling me to the bone. Thomas combed the streets of Quebec City, finding odd jobs as a day laborer so at least we had a little money to buy food. With this nourishment, we started to regain some of our strength. It helped to see Johneen begin to fill out again. His face lost that emaciated look, and he began to play with other children in the street by the tiny boarding house we'd found to rent.

There was a communal kitchen where I tried to learn to cook the local foods. There were a few familiar items, such as potatoes, but there was also wheat flour for flatbread called Bannock. Some women occasionally helped me, but I could never understand their French. Only one other woman in the house spoke English, and this was a bit easier since I had heard it sometimes in Ireland, so I tried to learn more of her words. The French language was rattled off so fast that I could never follow much of it.

Besides the shared kitchen, there was also a dining room with a real table and chairs. Johneen loved to climb onto the wooden chairs and swing his feet, and the joyful smile on his face warmed my heart.

Our bedroom contained only a straw-filled mattress on the floor, but this was just like our home in Ireland, and it became my retreat when all the newness around me became overwhelming. We'd been there several weeks when one day Thomas came in from work shoveling snow off city sidewalks and found me sitting on the bed crying.

"What's wrong, Maggie?"

"I miss our home so much," I sobbed. "Everything here is so strange. I can't understand a word of French, and even English is hard. Some days, I feel God has abandoned us and cast us into the outer darkness."

He sat down next to me and drew me into his arms. For a long time, he said nothing as I continued to cry. My breath came in ragged sobs until, at last, I had no tears or strength left. He stroked my back and kissed tears off my cheeks.

"It's been a long road," he murmured. "But at least we are alive, and not in watery graves. God has spared us for a reason, my dear one. I don't know what it is, but all we can do is wait and trust."

"That sounds like what Emilia says."

"Who is Emilia? Is she the woman who speaks English?"

My breath caught in my throat. *Oh my! How can I tell him she's a voice in my mind? He'll think I've gone daft.* "Yes, she speaks English," I muttered. *Is this a lie or not? I hear her in my thoughts, and I know I think in Irish. But she doesn't seem like a Gael, so perhaps she does speak English, and somehow I understand. Perhaps it's like that Day of Pentecost when all the different peoples heard their own language. The good Lord makes it so I can understand Emilia, and she can understand me.*

"I have trouble with French, too," Thomas said over my thoughts. "They talk so fast that I can't follow. Luckily there are a few fellows around who speak English. The French are Catholic, and I feel comfortable that we can even go to Mass here. Over to the west in Ontario, there is more English, but

I don't know if there are more Catholics or Protestants there. We must try to save a bit of our money in case an opportunity comes to go there."

A weight seemed to lift off my shoulders as he said this. "Yes, Thomas. I feel in my heart that Ontario might be a better place for us." These words were no sooner out of my mouth than he began to kiss me and caress my arms. As his hands moved down to lift my dress, I moaned, "Thomas, right here in a boarding house?"

"This is our own room. No one will disturb us here. I finally have the strength to love you. Please let me."

"Yes, this is a possible again," I sighed, relaxing into his caresses.

Later, after our light supper, I lay on my back in our bed, curled next to my husband. I felt a warmth that I'd thought was long-gone from my life. Johneen lay on the other side of me. It was good to sleep next to Thomas again.

As I looked toward the ceiling in the darkness, I searched my mind for Emilia. *Where have you been? Have you left me?*

'I'm sorry, Maggie. I have been working on something that I hope will help you. You seemed to be settling in here.'

I just can't get used to the Frenchwomen. I'm sorry.

'Don't be sorry. Something good is going to happen soon.'

What?

'I can't tell you now. Things have to happen according to the timing in your world. But please, don't give up hope.'

I tried to hang onto hope, but it was elusive. Part of it must have been the toll starvation and the terrible voyage had taken on my mind and body. Tears seemed to be waiting right behind my eyes, to break through at any moment.

* * *

Time dragged on after this. Even though we tried to save some of his wages, Thomas made just enough with day jobs to keep us fed, and the rent paid for our place in the boarding house. I tried not to get discouraged, but it appeared we would never get out of Quebec City. I felt like an outcast, for many of the French speakers tended to snub me because I couldn't speak their language. Winter also dragged, for the climate here in Canada was much colder than in Ireland. But I kept my tears and fears to myself as much as possible.

Then, after a couple of months, I realized I must be with child. My flows had stopped, and my emotions rose with each passing day. One evening, Thomas found me lying on our bed, sobbing.

"Maggie? What's wrong?" He sat beside me and began to rub my back in circles.

I brushed at the tears, but he'd already seen them. "I think I'm with child," I sighed at last.

A smile creased his lips. "That's not something to cry about. It's something to be joyful for. Just think Johneen will have a little brother or sister."

"I suppose so. But how can we afford another mouth to feed right now? And I feel so alone here. If only we could go to Ontario, where more people speak English. Sometimes the Frenchwomen are so rude because I can't understand them. I long to speak my own tongue again, my Irish."

He lay down alongside me and touched my belly softly. "Ah, there now, this is a gift from the Lord. He will send what we need to care for a wee babe." Then he took a deep breath before he spoke again. "I, too, would like to move on upriver to Ontario. I'll just have to find better-paying work. Somehow, we will get there."

"It all seems impossible, Thomas."

"Oh, I've heard the priest say, 'With God all things are possible.' Let's cling to that promise. I don't know how, but it will come to pass."

Days slowly began to lengthen as spring approached. The day in Ireland we called 'Saint Patrick's Day' arrived at last. Here people called it the Vernal Equinox, when the day and night were both twelve hours long—the first day of spring.

Even though there was a chill wind that night of March 21, 1848, we walked along the quay to watch the sunset. Johneen walked between us, holding each of our hands.

"Please swing me," he begged.

Thomas would count, "One, two, three!" and we'd grip his hands while swinging his arms so he flew between us, feet in the air, laughing at the top of his lungs.

After about a dozen swings, my arm was too tired, so Thomas put our son on his shoulders to mollify him. "We can't wear your mother out, son," he said. "After all, she's carrying your little brother or sister in her belly."

"Truly?" said Johneen. "Will I have another brother to replace Morgan?"

My eyes began to tear up as I thought of poor Morgan, buried all alone back in Ireland.

"Perhaps," said Thomas. Then he reached up and tickled the boy's tummy to distract him from the subject.

The sun barely hung above the water when a cold blast of wind hit us in the face. I turned my back to the gust, for it was taking my breath away. Now that I was getting close to four months along, the weight in my belly made it harder to breathe.

Thomas turned with me, placing one free arm across my shoulders. Johneen held himself in place with his arms on either side of his father's head. A man with a scraggly red-brown beard was walking toward us.

When he saw Thomas, he stopped. "Thomas? Thomas Cantlon?"

"Yes, I am. Do I know you?"

"What, you don't recognize your own brother? Well, I suppose I am a sight with all this beard."

"Patrick?" Disbelief filled my husband's voice.

The man pulled a woolen cap off his head, revealing an unruly shock of red hair. "Patrick Cantlon is my name," he said.

Thomas's eyes grew huge in surprise. "Patcheen? Holy Mary, is it really you?"

"Aye, Thomeen. None other. Just your long-lost brother."

Johneen began to bounce. "Who? Who?" Thomas set him down, and I grabbed the boy's hand so he wouldn't dash off.

As soon as his hands were free, Thomas grabbed the man by the shoulders. Then, he placed one hand in front of the beard. With the other, he pushed back the hair hanging over the man's forehead. "Why, as God lives, it is you Patcheen!" He pulled him into a firm hug.

"Don't choke me now, Thomeen. I've come a long way to find you."

Thomas stepped back but kept his hands resting on the other's shoulders. "Where have you been all this time? It's been—what?—over three years since you sailed from Cork?"

"Eighteen-forty-four," the man mused. "Something told me hard times were coming. There was an evil feel to the air."

"You must have the 'sight.' It began in forty-five, the potato blight. You would not believe the awful smell."

"Some say they heard the banshees crying on the wind the night it first came," I said.

"But you were about to give birth when I left in forty-four. Is this the lad born then?"

"Yes," nodded Thomas, "This is our John. We had another son in forty-five, Morgan—"

"But the Great Hunger took him," I murmured, trying not to cry. "So many died. And then they turned us out of our homes and knocked them down."

"Ah, Maggie. 'Tis almost a miracle to see you alive and well," said Patrick. "And in a family way, if I'm not mistaken."

"I barely show," I laughed. "You *must* have the 'sight'!"

"Come to our boarding house," said Thomas. "This cold will get worse now that the sun has set. Maggie and Johneen must get indoors."

We walked briskly away from the quay and into the front door of The White Swan, our boarding house. In the common room, a fire crackled in the hearth, and one chair near it was unoccupied. I sat down heavily and pulled Johneen onto my lap. Thomas and his brother stood with their backs to the fire so we could talk together. Hearing the sounds of Irish warmed my heart as much as the fire. The French people around the room paid us no heed as we chattered away.

"I have been working in the woods, over west in Ontario—Upper Canada, as most call it here." Patrick began. "I've been saving as much as I can, and I was going to send you passage money, but then rumors began to reach us about the evictions. I was afraid to send money and you not be there."

"That's probably what would have happened," said Thomas. "Do you have some special line to heaven that you know these things?"

"Oh, no. There were fellows in the camp who had heard of it from some who came on ships in forty-six."

"Black forty-seven was even worse," Thomas said. "The fever began to kill as many people as starvation. We set out in a group of five—an orphaned girl from our clachan, and a fellow we met on the road. But the ship fever took them both, and they were buried at sea. I say it's truly a miracle that our little family survived."

"Except for little Morgan, only one year old, who we had to bury coffinless back in Kerry," I added.

"But what made you come all the way back here to Quebec, if you were working in the lumber camps of Ontario?" Thomas asked.

"Well, that is a strange thing, I must say," said Patrick. "One night, it was like there came a voice in my head. It said I had to return here if I hoped to find you."

Oh, Lord, I thought. *This sounds eerily familiar.*

"Well, I thought at first I was crazy, like I'd had too much poteen."

"Ah, yes, the fire-filled whiskey made from fermented potatoes," said Thomas. "No one has made that for a long time, I guess. There weren't even enough potatoes to eat."

"That's what some of the new fellows in camp said. But that's not what I mean. This was more like a compulsion that wouldn't let me rest. Winter is the best time for lumbering, for the horses can skid the logs on sledges in the snow. When spring comes, everything bogs down in the mud. And when that finally dries, the wheels of wagons bump and bash in the ruts left behind."

"What do they do with the logs?" I was surprised to hear Johneen speak.

"Why, you are a sharp little fellow, aren't you?" Patrick laughed. "Well, we pile them on the riverbanks or lakeshores, right at the edges. Everything is iced over, of course. But when the spring thaw comes, the logs are gathered into great groups called rafts and floated downstream to the sawmills. If there aren't any mills built yet, they're loaded onto barges and boats to be shipped to where the nearest sawmills are. The rivermen who ride those rafts and keep them from jamming up have the most dangerous job of all lumbermen."

Johneen's eyes were wide in wonder. "I wish I could see those things."

"Perhaps you will." Patrick turned back to Thomas and put a hand on his back. "I believe that's why I'm here. You see, the passage money I'd been saving for you will be enough to take us upriver. What would you think about coming back with me to Ontario?"

"Oh, yes!" I blurted out. "We want to go to Ontario. Quebec is just too—" I stopped short of saying 'French', for some others in the room might hear me.

"Well, it's a long, long trip," said Patrick. "For me coming downstream wasn't so bad, but it will be upstream from here, up the St. Lawrence to Montreal. There, we move into the Ottawa River, which runs along the border of Ontario and Quebec. Our lumber camp is almost fifty miles upstream and inland on the Ontario side."

"But the river isn't still frozen?"

"No, brother. It's been open for almost three weeks now. Some say it's an early spring. But are you all up for the trip? It's a very wild country northwest of Montreal."

Thomas looked at me with concern in his eyes. "Perhaps we should wait until the baby is born?"

I felt my heart sink. "No, I don't want to wait. By that time, winter will be coming again. It could be another year before we could go. I can't wait that long. Johneen is going on four. He's growing into a strong lad. I'm sure we'll be all right. Do they need cooks in lumber camps, Patrick?"

"For sure. The cook is the most important person in the camp, and he needs several helpers. You wouldn't believe how much food those lumberjacks need to do their difficult jobs."

"Well, I've been learning to cook all kinds of things here besides potatoes. Perhaps I could work, too."

"If you're not busy taking care of a baby," said Thomas.

"Where there's a will, there's a way," I responded.

"Well, Patrick, you can see there's no arguing with my wife," he laughed. "When do you think we can get a boat heading upstream?"

"I'll start checking around first thing tomorrow." Patrick's face beamed. "It will be so good to be with family again after all this time."

"And to speak Irish," I said.

"Yes, but you'll have to learn English," said Patrick.

I moved closer to him and whispered, "It will be easier than French, I think."

Thomas found our landlady and asked if there was a spare room for Patrick. We were delighted when she said there was. "Old fellow moved out just two days ago," she said. "If he can pay, your friend can stay as long as he needs to."

"He's my brother," Thomas smiled. "And I'm sure he can pay." I was thankful that he didn't add that Patrick's stay might not be long—or that we might be leaving soon, too. After all, it would depend on finding a boat heading to Montreal.

That night, we all went to bed late. I was tired but too

excited to sleep. As I lay next to Thomas and stared toward the ceiling above me in the dark, I sought the girl in my mind.

This is your doing, isn't it, Emilia?

For what seemed a long time, there was no answer. I was about to ask if she'd left me for good when her voice finally came. 'Yes, that's why I had to be gone. It took a long time to find Patrick. It is very wild in the woodlands west of here. It won't be like anything you've ever known, Maggie.'

Yes, but I just have to get out of Quebec.

'I know. I did it for you. But somehow, I also know this is what I was sent here to do. Your future is not here in Quebec or even in Ontario. There's another place much farther west where your family will finally settle. It will be many years, and many miles. I don't know much more than that. Just that your destination, somewhere in the future, is in the United States, in the state of Michigan.'

You'll come with us, won't you?

'I'm not sure.'

But Emilia, it's almost like you're part of me.

'I'm one of your descendants, a hundred years in the future. It may be time for me to return to my life there. I don't know for sure yet.'

Tears welled into my eyes. *Please don't leave!*

'It's not my decision, Maggie. But I can tell you this. You are also a part of me. Your blood flows in my veins. And if you are in great need, I'm sure that blood will call me back to you.'

I hope so.

'So do I.'

Her voice whispered in my ear like she was right beside me.

CHAPTER 18
Interlude

Suddenly, everything went dark.

Cinda, what's going on? Where am I? A small circle of amber light appeared. As it grew, I felt a familiar warmth.

'You're back in your own time, Emilia—less than an hour after you left. Back in your own bed.'

But wait! I can't just leave Maggie out there alone, heading into the Canadian wilderness. She might need my help again.

'I'm glad you feel that attachment. That means you were the right person for this GAP-crossing,' said Cinda.

But it's not over. I need to know what happened to her, Thomas, and John.

'Well, I'm allowed to tell you some of it now. I'm sure you can guess one thing. After all, you are alive and breathing here in 2022, back in your home in Michigan.'

Her words puzzled me for a few moments. Then my thoughts gelled. *Since I'm alive, they must survive. At least John. He's my ancestor, isn't he?*

'Yes. John will become the father of your grandmother Mary Emilia Cantlon. He and his parents will slowly work their way across Ontario, following the lumber camps as they take the best timber. Much of it will be shipped to England and Scotland for shipbuilding. They will move from the Ottawa River to Lake Nipissing, where another river called the French River flows into Lake Huron. Once that area has been logged over, they will sail the North Channel of Georgian Bay in Lake Huron, eventually ending up in Sault Sainte Marie, Ontario.'

How many years will that take?

'At least thirty. By that time Thomas will be well on in years. When he can no longer handle the rugged woods work, he will have to stay behind in the camps and do what he can to help Maggie in the cook shanty.'

And Maggie? What happened to the child she was carrying?

'There will be a healthy boy they name Thomas. Maggie will be so determined to work that she'll strap the baby to her back while she works helping the camp cook. In time, her skills will be in great demand. The loggers are especially fond of her pies. Some days, she has to bake fifteen pies to keep those hungry men satisfied and strong for their grueling work.'

Lumbermen's Monument, Huron National Forest, Michigan. Left to right: Riverman with peavy, Timber Cruiser with compass, Lumberjack with double-bladed axe and crosscut saw. (Photo by M.F. Erler, May, 2024)

I've seen old photos of the men with their two-man crosscut saws working to take down a giant white pine. Others show a man with an axe, standing on a board wedged into the tree trunk, cutting the notch to direct the tree's fall. It must have been back-breaking work back then. Now, there are power saws and huge tractor skidders. With the advent of steam and then diesel power, the work shifted to wheeled vehicles, and the logging season became summer instead of winter.

'That's right, Emilia. I knew you were the person for this task because you are always studying and learning new things.'

Well, living in northern Michigan, the heritage of the great lumbering boom of the late eighteen-hundreds is all around me. Unfortunately, though, one of the legacies is mere remnants of scrappy woodlands that never fully recovered from being stripped of their best timber. Back then, people thought the supply would never run out. When one area was logged over, all they had to do was move west to the next one. No one thought there was a need to replant new trees for the future.

'Human beings have short lifespans which leaves them short-sighted about where their resources will come from when the ones they use up are gone. But back to your family story. Maggie and Thomas will have a little girl, too. They name her Margaret, after her mother. By the time the family reaches Sault Sainte Marie, which most locals just call *The Soo*, this daughter will be in her twenties. There in Canada, she will meet and marry a Scot named Ian McLeod.'

I've heard of that clan. Is he from the Isle of Lewis or the Isle of Skye?

'His parents emigrated in the early eighteen-hundreds from Stornoway on the Isle of Lewis.'

That's the Outer Hebrides, isn't it? I read they speak a Gaelic language similar to Irish there.

'Yes, several centuries ago, people from Ireland moved north to the Hebrides Islands off the west coast of Scotland. There, they developed a kingdom called Alba in those times.'

What about Thomas and Maggie's son, young Thomas?

'I'm sorry to say that he is killed by a falling limb while he is notching a large pine with his axe. They call those old dead limbs hanging overhead 'widow-makers.''

Oh, how sad! They will have lost two of their sons. But John must live, since I'm here.

'Right. Now, go to sleep, Emilia. Live your life here. Enjoy your years with your husband John Henry Parker. You will have grandchildren to enjoy. And in time, I will be born, but not for another fifty years or so. You see, I'm your great-great-granddaughter.'

That's right! I'd forgotten. My blood flows in your veins.

'Yes, just the way Maggie Cantlon's does in both of us.'

We are all products of those who came before, aren't we Cinda? Still, I wish I could see my great-grandfather, John Cantlon, as a man.

'Don't worry, you will. If things go right.'

The amber light winked out. For a while, I stared into the blackness where it had been, but at last, I fell asleep. When the morning came, I rose to go about my day, and everything seemed like it had been a long, strange dream.

* * *

Several months passed, and memories of Maggie started to fade from my mind. Then, one night, as I lay awake staring at the ceiling of our bedroom for hours, something in my mind kept niggling at me. I couldn't say precisely what it was, but it wouldn't let me sleep; it was as if it was something important that I needed to remember.

At last, a tiny amber light appeared above me, slowly descending toward my eyes.

Is that you, Cinda? What is going on? I feel so restless, like there's something important that I've forgotten to do. But I can't remember what it is.

'I'm sorry it's been so long, Emilia. The Time Guardian held me back. He said I mustn't interfere too soon, or the continuum would be upset.'

Who's the Time Guardian?

'You don't need to know. It doesn't concern you. My brother and I learned the hard way that there are certain limitations to what can and can't be done in time travel. You don't remember, but once, the Time Guardian had to correct a terrible mistake my brother Ian made.'

What was it?

'It doesn't concern you.'

The tone of her voice told me I had no business asking any more questions on that subject.

You have a brother named Ian?

'Yes, he's a few years younger than me.'

Is he related to the Ian McLeod, that man John Cantlon's sister married?"

'Only as a distant cousin. Remember, John is your direct ancestor. His sister isn't.'

Oh, yeah. So, is it time for me to go back to being 'within' Maggie?

'That was one of the things I had to discuss with the Time Guardian. He thinks it would be too stressful for you. Maggie has a difficult time in her later life.'

But her early life was difficult, too. I managed that.

'It's not the same. Anyway, this time, you will be 'within' another of your direct ancestors, John Cantlon's wife, Mary McLafferty.'

That sounds like a Scottish name.

'Yes, she was born in Scotland in 1864, and though many of her extended family moved to Ulster, Northern Ireland, she remained in southwestern Scotland, in an area known as Strathclyde.'

I remember seeing the River Clyde when I was a student in Scotland in 1970. It flows through Glasgow.

'Correct.'

Wait, Cinda. If she was born in 1864, that would mean that she is twenty years younger than John.

'Yes, he did a lot of moving with the lumber camps—remember? He didn't marry until he felt established enough. That wasn't unusual for Irish men in his generation. They faced many obstacles in getting work. Some companies posted large signs that said 'NINA'.'

What did that mean?

'No Irish Need Apply.'

How unfair!

'Yes, it was. Many other immigrant groups faced similar discrimination in the nineteenth century. But in the end, it made them strong in some ways. The Irish held on to their cultural heritage and banded together more than some other nationalities. They still have one of the strongest cultural identities even now.'

Isn't it strange how hard times can make people stronger?

'Sometimes, but not always. Some fall prey to dark depressions—like Maggie.'

Maggie?

'Oops! I wasn't supposed to tell you that.'

Is that why I can't go back to her? But perhaps I could help.

'That's not what is meant to be.'

Cinda, this is really frustrating! What is the point of my going back in these GAPs if I can't help?

'There is only so much you can do without upsetting the entire space-time continuum.'

Oh—

'But you can go now to be with Mary and John. They were married in 1882 in Sault Sainte Marie, Michigan. You will join them soon after this, and later, you will learn about his mother Maggie's fate from John.'

Michigan, did you say? Did they come to Michigan? My heart began to thump in excitement. *This will be closer to my home ground.*

'Yes, John crossed the St. Mary's River and settled on the Michigan side. It's there that he and Mary McLafferty met and fell in love. Mary was only eighteen, and John was thirty-eight.'

I hope they'll be happy, I say before realizing I was talking about the past.

'You will see for yourself, Emilia,' came Cinda's distant echoing voice.

Soon, I was whirling in a maelstrom of amber and orange light. I became dizzy, but there was nothing to grab to steady myself. Then I felt myself rising as if I was being pulled up into a twisting tornado. Turning, turning, then tumbling—and falling headlong into a dark red cloud.

$$\text{———}$$

CHAPTER 19

Awakened in 1884

For a moment, I was burning, and my skin was searing hot. Then, something pulled me back up, and a cool blue washed over me. I heard the sound of wild waters splashing over rocks. Then my feet hit the ground, and I stood looking into bright blue eyes. Soon, the rest of the face came into my view, and the curls of golden-red hair around his ears.

"Mary? Are you all right? You look like you've seen a ghost."

"No, I'm fine, John. For some reason, I just had a slight dizzy spell."

"Perhaps because you are with child?" he smiled.

"Oh, that I am for sure." I reached down and patted my belly, where it was beginning to protrude. "But it's nothing to worry about."

He stepped closer and put his arms around me. "We've been married two years now. For a while, it seemed there would be no child."

"God has his own timing, darling. Perhaps my womb wasn't ready when I was eighteen."

"Ah, forgive me for my impatience. Now that I'm over forty, I must confess I'm anxious to be a father, at last."

I reached my arms up and around him. "You're strong, John Cantlon. You have many years left to enjoy your life. How long did your father live? How old was he when he died? I never got to meet him—or your mother."

My husband stepped back, and a frown creased his face. "My parents, Thomas and Maggie, have been gone over thirteen years. You were a mere child when they died, and they weren't even sixty when it happened." He took a deep, shuddering breath. "Someday, I'll be able to talk about it."

This was the same answer I'd always received before. Something tragic must have happened if he still couldn't talk about it after all this time. I reached out and squeezed his hand. "Only when you're ready, dear. I'm sorry I asked again."

He shook his head so hard that I heard his neck crack. "This is a dark, deep pain. Perhaps if I let it out, it won't hurt so much. But right now, I have to go back to help Farmer Fritz with his haying. I'll be home for supper."

This was his summer job when the lumbering was shut down. As he strode away in the summer heat, my heart ached for him, as well as for myself. Having a husband twenty years my senior had its trials. There was so much more of life he had seen, and yet so much he wouldn't—or couldn't—tell me. He never spoke of his young life in Ireland during the Potato Famine. The Great Hunger had all passed years before I was born, though a few of my older aunts and uncles from Northern Ireland mentioned it in passing. One of them said it was much more devastating in the south and west of the Emerald Isle. "It was bad enough here," he said. "I hate to think what privations they faced in places like Mayo, Roscommon, and Kerry, which were among the hardest hit."

One day, while I was walking along the path in front of our lumber camp shanty door to ease the pain in my back, a red-haired woman came out of the shanty next to ours. "Hello,

I'm Maureen," she said. "My husband and I are new here. He's just started working in the woods this week. Where are you from?"

"I'm Scots-Irish—at least the rest of my family is. My husband is from County Kerry."

"Well, we came from Roscommon," she replied. "Things were desperate there. My brother and sister both died of the fever. My husband Sean and I fled for our lives. We had to go all the way to Dublin and take a packet boat across to Liverpool. It was all we could afford. They made us stand on deck for the entire voyage across the Irish Sea. The wind was bitter cold, and many of the weaker ones died right there on the deck. Poor Sean was one of the victims.

"After I got to Liverpool, I had to make do in the slums by the water. There, I met a kind German man named Eric, who took me in and married me. We stayed in Liverpool so long that both my children were born there. But now we've made our way to the wilds of Michigan."

I listened to the woman's story, remembering John telling me his family had come to Canada when he was only a small boy. He said all he really remembered was that the girl who shared his bunk on the ship had died of the fever.

"My mother covered my eyes when they tilted the board that sent her dead body into the sea, but I heard the splash. Later, my father was a lumberjack in the camps that worked their way west across Ontario for the next two decades. Mama was a helper in the Cook shanty. She worked much too hard. Perhaps that was why the darkness settled into her mind. Her smile disappeared, never to return. And her eyes lost their sparkle as she grimly moved through her work each day. When I was young, she sang the old songs as she rolled the dough and chopped the fruit for the dozens of pies she made a week. But as her hair turned gray in her early fifties, her mouth became a thin line, and there was no more music in her soul."

He never talked past that. All he said was that when eighteen-seventy came, there was a great drought and the woods in Ontario became tinder-dry.

* * *

At last, the day came for my lying-in. Labor had started hours before, and I tried to walk to ease the pains in my back. This worked until my water broke, and the fluid from my womb ran down my legs. I crouched in the doorway of our little cabin, crying out from the pain.

I heard footsteps running toward me. "Why aren't you in bed?" cried Maureen.

I was too breathless to reply.

Once the contraction momentarily eased, she helped me onto the mattress on the cabin's wood plank floor. I raised my knees with my feet close to my hips. It was time to push. There was no resisting it. She knelt between my legs.

"Yes, I see a head," she said. "Push hard!"

There was no need to tell me that, for I was already pushing as hard as possible. Suddenly, something gave way, and there was less pressure.

"The head is out." She reached up and pressed my belly. "Now for the shoulders. Take a deep breath."

I gasped in as much air as I could, and another scream escaped me. Again, the pain came and then went. Then I heard a loud cry. And this time, it wasn't my voice.

"It's a boy," said my neighbor. She held the baby up for me to see.

"Give him to me," I gasped. As soon as he was in my arms, I felt as if all the weight of the world had been lifted. My labors were over, and I had a son. I laid him across my chest and rubbed his little back. I could feel his breaths rising and falling. Soon, he was rooting, and I moved him to my breast.

I hadn't noticed anything except the baby, but the woman must have cut the umbilical cord. I did feel her press my belly again as I pushed out the afterbirth.

Once I caught my breath again, I murmured, "Thank you, Maureen. We've hardly had time to get to know one another since you arrived."

"Your husband is John Cantlon, right? My husband Eric has been working with him in the woods. Just yesterday Eric told me that you were getting near your time."

"I'm so glad you were here, Maureen. This is my first birthing, and I didn't even have time to find out if there's a midwife around."

"I don't think there has been one for several weeks now," she said.

I was beginning to notice my surroundings again and saw two young faces peeping in the doorway.

"Ma," said one, "May we see the little one?"

Maureen turned and asked me with her eyes. I nodded.

A young boy and girl slipped through the door and came to stand beside her. "These are my children, Anna and Timothy."

"What nice names," I said.

"Since my husband is German," she said, "he wanted their names not to be Irish."

I smiled at the children. "It's nice to hear new names." The girl, who was a little taller than her brother, returned my smile. I could see she had blue eyes and blond hair. Timothy was standing almost behind her and shyly glancing my way. His eyes were a greenish hazel color and his hair had streaks of brown amid the blond. I reached my hand toward him. "Don't worry, Timothy, I don't bite," I giggled. He cracked a small smile.

"What will you name your baby?" Anna asked.

"In my family, we usually name the firstborn son after his father, so I think he will be called John."

"Won't that be confusing?" This was the first time Timothy spoke.

"Oh, it will work if we call him wee Johnnie," I replied. "When he gets bigger, though, he won't be wee anymore."

"What does 'wee' mean?" asked Anna.

"Oh, I'm from Scotland, where it means 'little.' Though my husband is Irish, so he might want to call him Johneen."

"Does that mean little, too?" asked Timothy.

I could see Maureen smiling as I talked to her children, and I could tell she and I would become good friends. "My parents were Irish, son," Maureen said. "In Ireland, we add the 'een' when referring to someone very dear to us. Even if they're an adult."

"Oh, so your parents put it right in your name—Maureen—didn't they?" Anna said.

"Yes, I suppose they did." Maureen's voice cracked a bit, and I wondered if her parents were still living. I didn't want to ask, though. This was not the time for it. My mind shifted instead to my own family. Most of them were still back in Scotland and Ulster, and a letter rarely reached me. With the lumber camps moving so often, they were often several months old—if they reached me at all. I wondered if I should even try to write and tell them about my new baby. Perhaps even the letter telling of my marriage to John hadn't reached them yet.

All of a sudden, a great weariness swept over me, and tears began to drip down my cheeks. Maureen must have noticed, for she rose from where she was kneeling on the floor. "Go back to the cabin now, children. Mary needs to rest from her labor, and I must help her get cleaned up."

The two children disappeared through the door. I closed my eyes and let Maureen do whatever she felt necessary since I was too tired to help.

"Is there any family you need me to fetch for you, Mary?"

I shook my head. "I have none here. Just my husband."

"The same is true for me," she said.

I saw her walking toward the door with some red-stained cloths. Then I closed my eyes. I must have fallen asleep, for the next thing I knew, John was kneeling beside me, stroking my hair. "I love you, Mary," he said when he saw my eyes open.

The baby was stirring awake, too, and I moved him to my other breast. "I think we should call him Johnnie," I murmured.

"Johnnie is fine. He looks like it fits him well. You have performed a great labor. Bless you, my darling."

"Maureen, our nearest neighbor helped. She has two children, so she knew what to do."

"I'm sorry I had to be in the woods. But I have never been allowed at a birthing, so I would have been no help anyway."

"I hope we can stay here a while. Maureen and I could become friends."

"Well, I'll be helping Farmer Fritz with his autumn harvest. Then, the winter logging will soon get underway, so I think we can be here for a few months. I hear the winters here in Upper Michigan are much like Canada's. It will be good weather for skidding logs on sledges and piling them on the riverbanks. When the rivers thaw in spring, the peavy men move them downriver to the harbor on Lake Huron. Perhaps they will let me join that crew, and we can even stay the spring."

"I've heard that's dangerous work, John."

"All work is dangerous in the woods, Mary. I never told you that my brother, Thomas, died when a widow-maker limb fell on him."

Tears were seeping into my eyes again.

"Don't cry, Mary. It was years ago now. Many sad things have happened. I think that's what left my mother in such a dark place in her last years."

"I cry more easily when I'm tired. I'm sorry. Let's not talk of those things right now."

"Of course." He kissed my lips and then kissed the baby's dark head. "I wonder what color his hair will be?"

"Oh, you can never tell when they're born, I'm told. Many start as dark as coal, and then it falls out, and blond grows in. Same with their eyes. Most start with blue, but some later change to brown or green."

"It doesn't matter," John smiled. "He's our Johnnie, no matter what."

CHAPTER 20

The Tales Emerge

John worked hard through that long, cold winter as a lumberjack, and I split wood to feed our little iron stove, which sat in the middle of our cabin. I kept Johnnie's cradle close to the warmth, and sat in a wooden rocker beside it when I could and nursed him there.

Most of the time, though, I was at the sideboard, the only kitchen I had, kneading dough for bread or cutting meat off the deer carcass John had hanging outside the door. It was always frozen solid, for the outside temperature never rose above freezing. The meat was fried in a cast iron skillet set on top of the stove, while the loaves of bread were placed in an iron warming box beside it.

It was meager fare, but John only ate a light supper with us. For breakfast and lunch, he was in the camp's dining hall, where the camp cook served up vast amounts of food: pancakes, eggs, bacon, and potatoes for breakfast; huge helpings of hearty stew and lots of bread, with pies for dessert at dinner. The lumberjacks burned off all those calories working in the woods. I would have been a very round and fat woman if I had eaten that much.

In 1884, the observance of Christmas was a day off for the men and a celebration of extra food and festivities. The wives and families in the area could join in for a feast of turkey, cranberries, sweet potatoes, and pumpkin pie. A week later, on

January 1, 1885, when a blinding blizzard roared in, the men got one more day off. That day, there had been no plans for a special feast, but some of the men brought out their private stashes of whiskey and toasted the new year.

John, however, decided to stay home and celebrate quietly with us. I was thankful to have him there to give me a break from chopping and splitting wood for our little stove.

"I have much to be thankful for this year," he said, sitting on a wooden stool beside my rocker. "A son who bears my name and a beautiful wife."

"I do, as well, John. I have this lovely rocking chair you made for me with your own two hands."

"There is always plenty of scrap wood around," he said. "It was nothing."

"Oh, but you aren't here day after day, rocking and feeding a fussy baby."

He put his arm around my shoulders. "Your job is just as hard as mine, only in different ways. Where would I be without you, Mary?"

"I guess you'd be out carousing with the other men." I laughed.

"No, my father was never a lover of the whiskey, and I'm not either."

"I have this beautiful cradle you carved for Johnnie, too."

He closed his eyes for a few moments. "My father made a cradle for me, my mother told me. Their second son, Morgan, used it, too. But he died in the hard winter of forty-six and seven. There was bitter cold, snow, and not enough food. It's a miracle that the rest of us survived. My mother lay sick with dysentery most of the winter. Da must have, too, for all I remember is lying on the filthy straw mattress trying to keep warm."

"Those were terrible times, but now they're over," I whispered.

"Yes, we've begun to make a life here. We have enough to eat and warm clothes, but it's still hard. The winters here in Michigan are only a bit warmer than Ontario."

"I've been lucky to have Maureen next door," I said. "When she has a free moment, she comes over just to talk and keep me company. She doesn't talk about the famine, though. She says it's best forgotten because the pain and anger just comes back all the fiercer if she even thinks of it."

"My parents often said that, too."

I heard John take a deep shuddering breath before he spoke again. "I'm not like them, though. Some things I can't keep in my mind forever. If I do, I'm afraid they'll eat me from the inside out."

"Does it have to do with how your parents died?" I almost didn't ask this, for he'd never wanted to talk about it before.

Again, he took a deep breath and hissed the air out in a long whoosh. "I have to tell it," he said at last. "Maybe my parents were wrong about keeping all the hurt inside. I hope it will ease my mind to share it with you if you don't mind."

"Of course, I don't mind, John." I had finished nursing Johnnie, and he was sleeping in my arms. I considered putting him in the cradle but decided against it, in case he should wake. I didn't want anything to stop John from sharing his burden.

"Well, I've told you how we followed the lumber camps up the Ottawa River. Gradually, we moved upriver and a bit further inland into Ontario. Logs were piled by the frozen rivers that fed the Ottawa as we do here on the Pine River. In spring, the rafts of logs are floated down to the boat docks to be ferried to the sawmills further downstream. Spring came early in 1870. The rivermen had the logs downriver by June.

"We began burning the slash—all the leftover limbs and scraps of unusable wood. The sawmills only wanted the best, especially the white and red pine. No one told us when or where to burn. We just piled all the slash as best we could and set it afire. Down along the Ottawa River, some were clearing fields to farm, so they were burning slash there, too. And in order to really plow the fields, they also had to burn out the stumps.

"The usual rains didn't come that spring and summer, and the grasses and brush became so dry it crackled when you walked on it. I was young then, just past twenty-five, so I was one of the pilers and occasionally got to light a slash pile. Things were so dry that the flames from those burning piles leapt higher than I'd ever seen before. But no one said it was the wrong time to be burning in the woods. In fact, some liked that the piles burned fast and had to be tended less. In wet springs and summers, we would have to keep nursing those fires along, or they'd go out before all the slash was burned.

"By August of that year, though, dry winds began to blow in from the west. One day, three of our burning piles flamed so much that they merged together. A couple of us tried to haul buckets of water to douse the raging flames, but it was no help. The winds gusted stronger as each hour passed, and before long many piles were no longer separate. There was a continuous wall of flames racing toward the Ottawa River.

"All we could do was try to get out of the way. I ran as fast as I could toward the logging camp, but the fire beat me there. By the time I arrived, all the shanties, including the cookhouse and dining hall, were burned to the ground. There were a few burnt bodies amid the hot ashes, but it was impossible to tell whose they were. So, I never got to bury my parents. But they must have died in that fire, for I never saw them again. They ended like my brother Morgan with no gravesite, coffin, or stone to mark that they'd ever lived. At least my brother Thomas is buried somewhere in Ontario. And my sister Margaret had married and moved west in Canada with her husband. I don't even know where she is."

By now, tears were dripping down my husband's cheeks. I wasn't sure what to say, so I just placed my free hand on his arm and gave it a gentle squeeze.

"They just call it the Great Fire," he murmured. "The survivors picked up and moved on, following the timber. Every spring, they still burn the slash, rain or not. Farmers still clear the forests to make farm fields. The forests are disappearing. I hear the next year, 1871, the drought moved south into the lands around Lake Michigan, and on one fateful night, October 8, 1871, the city of Chicago burned to the ground. Later, news reached the world that one and a half million acres had burned in northern Wisconsin and wiped out a little town called Peshtigo. Almost two and a half million acres burned in Michigan, too, taking out three cities, two in the west and one far to the east in the state."

"That seems so eerie that all three of those catastrophes happened in one night."

"I know. People in those places thought the end of the world had come."

"If I had been there, I would have felt the same, John."

"Now, as I look back, all I see is a black, scorched land in my mind. The lumber barons take what they want, burn the land, and move on. No one knows if a new forest will ever grow, and it seems no one cares. There's always more timber to the west. Here in Michigan, it's the same. They logged off the lands below the Straits of Mackinac and then moved up here. We keep on marching westward. I hear there's big timber across Lake Michigan in Wisconsin and across Lake Superior in Minnesota.

"Almost every year, some farmer's fire or lumber slash fire gets away and burns land and often homes. I wonder if people will ever change their ways and think of the earth, instead of just themselves. Will this go on forever?

"It reminds me of stories my mother said her granny told her—tales of how the Gaels kept getting pushed to the west of Europe, across Britain and Ireland, until we met the broad Atlantic Ocean. There was no place to go from there, but to cross the seas. And here we are, in what was called the New World, still pushing west, and leaving a trail of wasteland behind us. Will it ever end?"

We both sat in silence for a long time after he stopped, listening to the soft crackling of the warm fire in our stove. *How ironic,* I thought. *Fire is such a help and comfort to us. It warms our home and cooks our food. Yet, it's a terrible monster when it gets out of control.*

'That's true,' came a quiet voice in my head.

What? Who are you? Am I crazy and losing my mind from hearing all of John's sad stories?

'No, Mary. Don't be afraid. I'm one of your descendants. My name is Emilia. A time traveler sent me to live 'within' your mind for a while. I won't be born until about seventy years from now, in 1952.'

My heart began to pound. *Seventy years? Why are you here?*

'I'm not sure yet. There must be something coming up where a decision must be made about which path to take. Perhaps I'm here to help you choose.'

Help me choose what?

'The path that will lead to me, to the descendants you're supposed to have. I wish I knew more, but they say I'm not meant to.'

Who are they?

'I'm told they are called Time Guardians. That's all I know.'

The voice faded, and I heaved a deep sigh. John looked over at me and frowned. "Have I upset you? I'm so sorry."

"No, dear. I'm glad you could share these hurts with me. Now I pray they won't weight you down, and you can live a better life."

"Yes," he nodded. "I want a better life for you and our children than wandering around, following the logging camps. Maybe I should try farming. Or something else, something where we can find a place to settle down and have a home. I haven't had a place to call home since my parents brought me from Ireland almost forty years ago. I don't want our children to live like that."

"Is there a town we can go to and see what opportunities are there?" I wondered if this was my own question, or something I was hearing from the voice in my mind.

"The closest town to us right now is Sault Sainte Marie," he said. "Perhaps I can collect what I'm owed for this year's work, and we can buy a wagon to head there. I hear there is a trail that leads back to the town."

"Yes, John. Let's try that."

CHAPTER 21
Choices to Be Made

In the Spring of 1885, our two-wheeled cart John managed to build rolled into the village of Sault Sainte Marie, Michigan. This was the upper peninsula of the two that made up the state of Michigan. People in Upper Michigan just called it the U.P. Though we were far north, the hottest days of summer were beginning.

Poor John had to push the cart most of the way. After he'd cobbled it together from scrap lumber in the camp, a fellow lumberjack named Sven had offered to walk the first several miles with us, leading a pony he'd bought the year before. To keep the load light, I walked most of the time too, holding onto the cradle, which had been carefully packed near the top of the load. This way, I could lay Johnnie in it when he was asleep. Other times, I carried him, especially when nursing. Occasionally, John would set him on his shoulders, but the baby was too small to sit up there for long, and soon his little back would sag. At times, he leaned forward and rested on top of John's head.

"I remember riding on Da's shoulders often," he'd say. "I was older but probably light as a feather because of the famine. Good thing, though, for Da was weak and emaciated himself."

"I still believe 'tis a miracle that you survived it all," I said. And in my heart, I wondered if the strange girl in my mind, Emilia, had anything to do with that.

When we'd gone about halfway to the town, Sven had to take his pony and return to camp. "I can't miss another day of work. I'm sorry," he said. "But I wish you well, There are others of us who would like to find a new kind of work as well. You're very daring to set off like this, especially with a young family." He nodded to me with a small smile.

"Ah well, my parents dared even more than this when they set out to walk fifty miles to Cork and set sail on a ship, not knowing if they'd even survive the journey. They had no choice then. But I am making this choice to honor their courage and their memory."

"Godspeed to you then, my friends." Sven shook our hands, and then he and his pony turned back down the rough trail toward the camp.

Ahead of us, the trail was wider and a bit smoother. It must be traveled more than the rugged path to the lumber camp. I was thankful for John's sake; now, he stood between the poles previously hitched to the pony. I carried Johnnie most of the time now, except when he slept, then I rested my aching back by putting him in the cradle for short periods.

So we reached Sault Sainte Marie. There were only a few wooden buildings lining the main street and the few cross streets, for even though it was the oldest town in Michigan, it was not a city. The town across the river in Canada was larger. Along the southern edge of the St. Mary's River was the canal dug in the 1850s.

We stopped for a break and surveyed the canal. "You know this was mostly dug by Irishmen," said John. "Most of them were still starved from the Famine, and many died of sheer exhaustion. That canal was built with Irish blood, and now the ships have a way around the falls for convenience. Boats used to have to unload their cargo before the falls and load it onto trams, which carried it across to be reloaded onto boats on Lake Huron. Now they just pass through the canal."

"How do they keep from having fast water running downhill?" I asked.

"That's what the locks are for. They sail into a lock chamber, the upper gates are closed, and the water in the lock is dropped to the level of the next section of the canal. Then the lower gates are opened, and the boat sails right on."

"It's like a series of stairsteps then."

He nodded. "I wonder if they need any workers at the locks. Perhaps I should ask."

"Maybe we need to find lodgings first," I said.

"Oh yes, of course. You must be very tired, my dear."

I barely nodded, not wanting to complain.

* * *

We found a boarding house a couple of blocks from the locks. Our room even had a small window. If I looked to the north, I could see the mist rising from the St. Mary's Falls and hear the rumble of the water as it splashed and crashed over the rocks. I found it a pleasant, calming sound. In the house's common dining room, people spoke both French and English. At least I spoke English and a few French words. Yet, I already missed Maureen and her friendly smile.

After a few days, John found work at a small sawmill that had recently been built. The logs for it were not from our old camp, which floated theirs down the Pine River to Lake Huron. These came from the south shore of Lake Superior in northern Wisconsin.

Since the mill was just starting, however, the pay was low, and we had barely enough to get by.

"I need to find something better," he said. "If we can't earn enough to save, we'll never be able to afford a place of our own. I don't want you to lead the tenant-farmer life my parents were forced into. There must be something better."

One afternoon, while Johnnie was napping, I decided to walk along the lane in front of the boarding house to get some fresh air. Of course, there was still the smell of the rubbish and human waste along the gutters of the streets. There was no escaping this, but I breathed through my mouth to avoid some of the stench. I hadn't walked far when I came across a woman in a long buckskin dress leaning up against the wall of a building. Her legs were stretched out across the walkway, so I had to jump across the gutter into the snowy street to avoid them. My feet slid on the icy slush, and I fell.

"Oh—oh!" the woman cried. "Sorry." She jumped up and helped me to my feet.

I saw the same weariness and hopelessness in her eyes that I felt. She didn't speak as I said, "Aye, alright, ta." Then I realized I'd spoken too fast in my Scottish-English.

Her face became confused.

"Oh!" I patted my chest. "Okay now."

She smiled at this. She must know a little English, like I did. I pointed to myself and said, "Mary."

She nodded and pointed to her chest, and said, "Naweona." Then she added, "Chippewa."

Now I knew what I had suspected—she was a member of the Sault Chippewa Tribe. They were not a large group, for I had heard many of them had been forced to move west onto a reservation in Minnesota Territory.

"This your home?" I said, motioning my arm around the lane.

"No." She pointed down to where the lane narrowed and faded into a small woodland. "Wigwam there. You visit me?"

I could see that she was feeling isolated and alone like I was. My heart went out to her, and I wanted to follow her right then, but Johnnie was asleep up in the boardinghouse bedroom, and I couldn't leave him alone any longer.

I had a motion of rocking a baby and pointed back toward the door of the boarding house, shaking my head. "Another time?"

She looked disappointed at first, but then her eyes brightened as she understood my meaning. "Later?" she said. "Maybe next day?"

Seeing the hopeful look in her eyes, I nodded. "Yes, Tomorrow morning." I made a sign with my hands to show the sun rising.

Her face broke into a smile. "Yes. Bring baby, too."

This was the beginning of an unusual but meaningful friendship for me and, I think, for Naweona, too. With her broken English and many hand signs, we began to share our life experiences with each other. When she talked of how the white Europeans were gradually taking their native lands from them, I would often cry. As I tried to explain what had happened in Ireland—how the English had gradually pushed the Irish off their lands and made them their tenants on land that had belonged to their forefathers, she nodded in understanding. I told her this had happened in my native Scottish Highlands, too.

"The land does not belong to people," she told me. "People belong to the land. It is our life, our blood. The spirits of our ancestors are here, in each tree and animal." She wasn't able to say this all at once in English, but over the course of time, I could tell what she meant.

I always took Johnnie on walks with her into the woodland, and one time she pointed to a particular tree. "This my grandmother's tree," she said.

I did my best to tell her that the native Irish and Scots felt the same bond to their land. We began to realize that both of us were victims of the same colonial attitudes—that we, as natives, were thought of as inferior to the new people who pushed us aside. The Chippewa were being forced west, just as our people had been. My heart ached as I wondered if these native people would reach a great ocean and face nowhere else to go—as so many Gaels had.

Naweona had a little girl named Wainone who seemed about four years old. She came along with us on these wanderings. She would point to footprints in the snow and say names the of animals who had made them in her language. Her mother would do her best to interpret. At times, Wainone would hop like a rabbit or scurry like a squirrel to show what animal she meant. We all began to learn to communicate, using Chippewa and English.

One morning when Johnnie and I arrived at Naweona's wigwam, we saw all her belongings piled in baskets beside the rounded entrance. "What's happening?" I asked.

"The whites are trying to force our Sault tribe to move to Minnesota again," she said, tears dripping from her eyes. "We are going to cross the rushing water to Canada. Hopefully, they will not be able to reach us there."

"But won't the people over there want you to give them your land, too?"

"Sometimes the Canadians are less greedy for our land, and our chief is more powerful there." She pulled me into a tight embrace. "Our only hope is there."

By now, tears were flowing down my cheeks. "Oh, Naweona, I will miss you."

She stepped back and nodded. "We are friends. When the Great Spirit comes to protect all his children, we will meet again."

I put my hands on her shoulders and stroked her long black hair. "Yes, friends forever."

As I stepped away from her, I saw little Johnnie give her a smile.

Naweona moved quickly to take her daughter's hand. "Must go now. Before they come to take us away." Her daughter nodded, and they began to put the baskets on their backs, held by leather thongs. As we watched, they slipped out the wigwam's door and looked up and down the path. Then, they began to walk and soon disappeared among the woodland trees. They were so quiet; I never heard a twig snap or a soft footfall.

* * *

One evening after this, another man in the boarding house sat beside us at supper. He introduced himself as Edward. "I hear you are looking for land," he said.

"Yes, we are," nodded John. "How did you know?" I could see a cautious look in his eyes.

Edward ignored this question. "I hear there's farmland opening up west of here," said Edward. "It's near a place called Newberry. The loggers have already cleared it, and the ground is rich and dark. They're selling it cheap, only a dollar an acre."

John glanced at me and raised his eyebrows. "How far is this land from here?"

"About sixty miles, I'm told."

"So you haven't been there, Edward?"

"Not yet, but a few of us are getting a small group of wagons together to head there in the fall. It's the best time to travel, they say. The ground isn't wet like spring, and it's not snowing yet."

"We don't have a horse or anything to pull a cart. And our cart is small, only a two-wheeler."

"I have a four-wheel wagon with a cover, pulled by two horses. Since it's just me, I could make room for you and your wife and child."

"I don't know." Thomas scratched his chin. "Seems like a long way to go before winter sets in. Snow can start anytime from mid-September. I'm not sure it would be good for such a young baby to travel in the cold."

"Oh well, if you're not interested, I'll keep looking around," Edward said. He rested his eyes on me for several seconds. Something sent a chill through my arms and legs.

'He has designs on you,' said the voice in my head.

Emilia, you're still here?

'Oh, yes. And this is exactly what I'm here for. This man is a kind of huckster for the men in Newberry who want to unload poor farmland on unsuspecting immigrants. That land, which looks so dark and rich, is really peat bogs. One year of plowing will dry it out, and all that will be left is barren sand.'

You're sure about this?

'It's history in my time, Mary.'

By this time, Edward had walked to another table across the room and sat next to another young couple. He glanced back at me once and winked, which made me feel very uncomfortable.

"I don't like the way he looks at you," John whispered in

my ear. "I would never feel right sleeping in his wagon, even if it had featherbeds."

"I agree. Let's go up to our room. There must be other options for us than farming."

Once we were in our room and the baby was settled for the night, we sat on the bed and talked in soft voices, so as not to wake him.

"Farming was a losing enterprise in Ireland for my parents," said John. "They barely had enough to pay the rent, and some years it went unpaid. They never had enough to eat. I was very young, but I could see the strain in their faces, especially after the potato blight came. I really don't want to be a farmer. But I have heard of another possibility or two."

"What have you heard?"

"Some of the men at the sawmill talked of iron ore and copper discoveries in the western part of this U.P. They say a man can make a living wage mining, and some of the companies even provide houses for their workers."

"But mining must be so dangerous, going into those tunnels underground. What if they cave in?"

"Logging was dangerous, too. Remember the fires? And how Thomas died from that widow-maker?"

"And always moving," I added.

"Yes, that's why we left. I thought of trying to be a riverman, guiding the rafts of logs downstream, but that was the most dangerous job of all. Logs would jam, and men in their calk-boots would have to run across the logs with a peavy, a rod with a sharp point on the end, to try to push the logs apart. But logs could roll and throw a man into the water, or he might be crushed between logs ramming together. It was another bad way to die."

I sighed and put my head in my hands. "I guess there really aren't any jobs that aren't dangerous, are there?"

"Not for us immigrants," he said. "At least not until we've become part of the main population of this new country, America. But it was even worse back in Ireland. There was no way for an Irish Catholic man to improve his lot. At least here, there's a chance."

"So what should we do, John?"

"I think that once winter is over, we somehow get a wagon and horse of our own and head west. There's a city called Marquette where they load the iron ore into ships to sail Lake Superior, through this canal here at the Soo, and down Lake Michigan to steel mills by Chicago. Or down Lake Huron and through Lake Erie to mills in Cleveland, Ohio."

"This land, this country is so big," I sighed. "I miss my little bit of Scotland."

"I'm sure you do." He gave me a long hug. "But this big country means bigger opportunities. I don't want to just sit here and let them pass me by. Either I mine the ore, or I help load the ships. I've had plenty of practice already unloading timber for the sawmill. All this lumber is loaded onto other ships and taken to places where people are building new houses and settling new lands. We need to become a part of that somehow."

CHAPTER 22
Trying to Head West

John labored two more years at the sawmill, and we scrimped every penny we could. There just never seemed to be enough to afford a horse. Our two-wheeled cart was all we had, but it would do the job, for we had so few possessions. The bed and dresser belonged to the boarding house. All we had was the rocking chair and the cradle, but John would no longer pull it alone.

When 1886 dawned, I discovered I was with child again. John acted overjoyed, but my heart sank. "How can we think of traveling now?" I moaned.

He drew me into a warm embrace. "My job is still secure. The Lord must mean for us to stay here a bit longer."

"But we want to get a place of our own."

"Someday we will, but we must wait. The men I work with are good fellows. You have made a few friends here."

Tears slipped from my eyes, and he wiped them off my cheeks. "I suppose you're right, John. There must be a reason we are staying here longer than we planned."

"There is no way to plan in a world like this," he said. "We must wait upon the Lord."

I caught my breath in surprise. "I heard Marie, the woman I do washing with, say something like that just the other day."

"What was it?"

"She said it was a verse in the Bible. 'They that wait upon

the Lord will renew their strength.' Those were the words she told me."

"I wish we had a Bible. I never saw one outside the Parish Hall," John sighed. "My family came from Ireland with nothing but the clothes on our backs and just fortunate to be alive."

"And we never had a Bible, either. The Catholic church didn't seem to make them available like I heard the Protestants did."

"Still, I'm not ready to leave our mother church," said John. "It's the one spiritual rock in our lives. I can't imagine abandoning it."

"Oh, I agree. Perhaps I can ask Marie if she knows where I can get an English Bible. It could be a comfort to read when times are hard."

He looked at me in surprise. "Do you mean you can read? I never learned how."

I was embarrassed that he said this. It had never occurred to me that my husband couldn't read. I couldn't think of what to say except, "I'm sorry if I embarrassed you, John. I didn't know."

"I was only three years old when my family was forced to flee Ireland. I never had a chance to go to school. My parents couldn't teach me because they didn't know how to read, either."

I reached up and stroked his chin, where his beard was beginning to show some gray whisps among the reddish-brown. "You're an intelligent man and a good provider. That's all that matters."

"Well, at least now I know that you can read, I hope you can get one of those Bibles and read things to me. By the way, when do you think your time will be due?"

"I'm guessing about six months from now."

"That will be shortly after Christmas, won't it?"

I nodded. "Perhaps when spring comes next year, we can begin to travel west. The baby will be old enough by then, I hope."

He smiled and pulled me into another hug.

* * *

This second birth was easier, and there was a midwife who came to help. As I passed through labor, I remembered Maureen and how kind and helpful she had been when Johnnie was born. Just over two years had passed since we left that lumber camp, and I wondered where she was and how she and her dear children were doing. But there was no way to know.

When my baby finally emerged, the midwife announced I now had a daughter. I was settled with her at my breast, and the bedroom had been put back into order by Marie and the midwife by the time John got home from work. He peeked in the bedroom door shyly, and I smiled up at him.

"Come see your daughter, darling. She's such a little doll. And I think she's going to have your red hair."

"What do you think we should name her?"

"I think Clara is a pretty name."

"It reminds me of County Clare," he smiled. "It was north of where I was born in County Kerry. What about a middle name?"

I thought for only a moment before I said, "Maureen. Yes, Clara Maureen Cantlon."

"I like the sound, Mary. Wasn't Maureen the neighbor who helped you when Johnnie was born?"

I nodded. "For some reason I kept thinking of her while I labored."

He sat on the edge of the bed and stroked little Clara's head. "She is our Christmas present this year, isn't she?"

"Is it Christmas? I lost track. It was all I could do to keep track of Johnnie and wonder when my labor would start."

"Today is Christmas Eve," smiled John. "And it looks like we're in for a snowy blow. Sometimes, when it snows, I have bad memories of how cold we were in the winter of forty-six back in Ireland. But now I'll have a good memory to think on instead—the birth of our little Clara Maureen."

"Christmas tomorrow? That means you will have the day off?"

"Yes. We can just snuggle and be warm here in our little bedroom. But where is Johnnie?"

"Marie took him to play with her two boys, to keep him out of the way. Besides, you know as well as I do that a birthing is no place for a man—or boy—to be."

John just nodded. Then he leaned over and kissed my forehead. "I'll take him down to the kitchen and find a bite for supper. Do you want us to bring you anything?"

"Perhaps just a little warm broth, if there is any. When Clara finishes her supper, I hope to get some sleep myself."

***

As 1887 dawned, the blizzards came one after another. I was thankful we were not trying to travel or that John had to work in the woods. One morning, while I was nursing Clara, there came a tap at the door. Johnnie rushed over to open it. There stood Marie with a book in her hand.

"I couldn't get this in time for Christmas," she began. "But you were busy, anyway."

"You could say that." I smiled as she stepped closer to where I sat in the rocker. I don't need a gift. I have nothing to give you."

"Not to worry. I have enjoyed your little boy. He's a sweetheart."

"I'm glad he hasn't been a bother."

"Oh, he and my Willie and Teddy get along so well. He keeps them out of trouble so I can get my chores done." Then she set the black book on my lap.

When I saw the lettering on the cover, I gasped. "A Bible! Oh, Marie, it must have cost you too much."

"Worth every penny," she replied. "Besides, I know it will be a blessing to you. Your husband told me how much you wanted one."

"He does, too. Do you know that he was only three when his family fled Ireland? He was never able to go to school. Now, perhaps I can teach him some things from this Bible."

"I know you want to head west with the spring," said Marie. "I pray this book will give you the strength and hope you will need. It's a wild and dangerous world beyond this little city of Sault Sainte Marie."

"Yes, I've heard it from many others. We will need the protection of the Blessed Virgin Mary on our journey."

She gathered my hands in hers. "Even though we will have to part in a few short months, you will always be in my heart and my prayers, Mary Cantlon."

Tears filled my eyes, and all I could do was nod.

* * *

Spring finally came to the far north corner of Michigan in late May. Johnnie was now three and becoming a good helper for both his parents. Clara was already almost six months old, babbling and trying to scoot on her tummy.

One Friday, we were sitting on the stoop and enjoying the sunny warmth when Johnnie jumped up and ran to where his father was approaching. I stood and saw right away what he was so excited about. John was leading a dappled gray horse.

"Glory to God!" I cried. "Is it really ours?"

"Oh, yes, she is," John laughed. "This sweet old mare is called Patti. A fellow at the mill sold her to me for this week's wages. She shouldn't have any trouble pulling our little cart."

"When do we go, Da?" Johnnie was jumping up and down.

"I've given notice at the mill, so we can leave in a week."

"Oh, a whole week…"

John laughed at Johnnie's disappointed voice. "Your mother needs time to pack, son. And we also have to let the landlady know when we plan to leave her boarding house."

Clara must have picked up on her brother's excitement, for she began to squeal with laughter. I smiled and stood, walking over to John. He patted the mare's withers, and she shook her head. "She's strong but gentle," he said. "We won't have to worry about her nipping at the children—or us. Our cart will hardly seem a load to her."

"What good fortune that your coworker wanted to sell her. Did he say why?"

"He's going to start working on the railroad bridge."

"You mean the one connecting this Michigan side to the Sault Sainte Marie in Canada?"

"Yes, they just began it when winter broke. He said he would be working on the Canadian side and couldn't take the horse across with him."

"Well, all I can say is praise God. And I'd better start thinking of what we'll need. Somehow, we must get some food supplies to take with us."

John smiled and pulled a wadded-up bag of coins from his pocket. "I'm squirreling away every extra penny. This will get us started."

"If only the railroads were done instead of just being built," I sighed.

"Train tickets are expensive, Mary. But I've come up with a better plan. Instead of working our way across through the lumber camps, I'm going to work on the railroad. There's one already started leading from here to Marquette. It will be a hard place for a family to live, but all we can do is try."

'Don't worry, Mary. There will be a couple of other wives you can meet.'

Emilia, is that you? I thought you'd gone again.

'I was working on getting that horse for you.'

Oh, God bless you! What is this place called Marquette like?

'It's another town like this one. It was also founded around forty years ago, so at least it won't be one of those wild frontier towns where there is no law. Some of them are real hellholes.'

Why do you keep helping us like this?

'Well, I confess I have a personal interest. Your next daughter will be my ancestor—my grandmother, in fact.'

My next daughter? I'm going to have another? When will that be?

I've already told you too much. Just forget what I said, and live your own life.

How long will it take us to get to Marquette?

'It will be quite a while. But don't worry. I'll do my best to make sure you get there.'

CHAPTER 23

Working On the Railroad

The railroads in Upper Michigan were often a haphazard affair. Each timber or mining company would run its own line to the nearest shipping port on Lake Superior or Lake Michigan. Since we wanted to move toward Marquette, we did our best to find the lines heading toward Lake Superior. It was a long, arduous process.

A line was run north to a port on Superior called Grand Marais, but that one turned to disaster when the first locomotive to run on the track was thrown off because a section of the roadbed gave way. The company gave up, deciding the underlying land was too unstable for a railroad. They went back to hauling by wagons in summer and sledges in winter.

John had spent almost five years on this job, and we were discouraged when we had to reload our cart, hitch up our aging gray mare, and move further west. The next line we encountered was trying to make its way to a small port on Lake Superior called Munising.

Building a railroad was much more than laying ties and tracks. First, surveyors had to determine the best route through the rocky terrain. Then, deep cuts had to be blasted through cliffs. The railroad grade could not be too steep for the locomotives to pull their loads uphill, and the downhill stretches had to be leveled off to prevent runaway trains. Bridges were needed over every river and stream, and huge trestles of wood were built to cross deep valleys.

Once these jobs were completed, which often took a year or more, the heavy wooden ties had to be hauled in and placed. At last, the track was ready for the steel rails. These had to be straight and evenly spaced to prevent cars from derailing. One of Johnnie's favorite things to do was watch the Gandy Dancers set the rails in their exact alignment. Each man in the crew used a five-foot-long iron lever called a gandy. They had to work as one to ensure no bends in the rails. A 'call man' would keep them in rhythm with songs and chants as they pushed the rail into place with a loud "huh!" and a dance-like movement.

Once a section of rails was in place, a locomotive could move up the track, bringing more materials to begin building the next section. Johnnie, and when she was old enough, Clara, would dance and sing as the locomotive arrived. They had learned some of the songs the workers used and would often chant:

> *"I've been working on the railroad all the livelong day.*
> *"I've been working on the railroad, just to pass the time*
> > *away..."*

Another one Johnnie liked was about the men who drilled into the rock to blast the cuts through the cliffs that blocked the way:

> *"Drill, ye Tarriers, drill.*
> *Well, it's work all day for sugar in your tay,*
> *Down along the railway.*
> *So drill, ye Tarriers, drill!"*

John had to work on most of these projects, all except for the surveying, since he couldn't read. I had been teaching him a few words when we read from the Bible each evening at bedtime. But some nights, he was so exhausted that he fell asleep before I could finish a passage.

Five years passed. I saw my husband build strong muscles from the strenuous work, but I feared for his life many times, especially when they were blasting or when he was high in the air, helping place timbers to hold up a trestle. I did my best to keep my fears from Clara, now almost four, and Johnnie, approaching five.

As 1889 dawned, winter waned early, which was a great blessing, for I was with child again. We were housed in a shanty, as usual, in one of the railroad company camps. This time, the tracks were supposed to be heading for Marquette at last. I had made a new friend named Veronica in this camp. She said her family had come to America from northern Italy two generations ago. Her English was very good since she had been born in New York City. I learned some New York slang words and even a few in Italian.

She was the one who revealed to me some of the privations immigrants from all parts of Europe entering the port of New York City had endured.

"There were always runners and hucksters at the docks, my grandfather told me. They would grab your luggage and promise you the best rates in town. But they were actually charging double. Once they had their hands on your luggage, there was no getting it back, so the price had to be paid. Some people stayed in the city but ended up in squalid tenements. My grandfather said that at first, their living conditions were worse than anything they had experienced in Italy."

"I wonder how the Irish fared?"

"Some say they were treated even worse. There were few

jobs that would accept them. Most ended up laying sewer lines or building subway tunnels, bridges, and tram lines. These were the most dangerous jobs, and many men died.

"At last, my father said, 'Enough is enough!' We headed up the Hudson River to Albany, where he got work on the Erie Canal. It had been finished in 1825, and canal men were in demand."

"What year was that?"

"I think my father said it was 1847."

"That was about the time many Irish were fleeing the Potato Famine in Ireland. My husband said his family came in Black '47, but they came through Canada. He was almost four years old, so he doesn't remember a lot, except that many people were starved and sick, and thousands died."

"Well, coming up the Hudson and across the Erie Canal to Buffalo, a great many more immigrants—especially Irish—were being swindled. Again they were charged higher fares and double rates on their baggage by many unscrupulous men. Your husband's family were probably lucky they came through Canada."

"I don't know. We have met many Irish who left Canada for the United States as soon as possible," I said. "They hoped for better opportunities here. The work is hard, but my husband, John, has done all right for us. He's been a lumberjack, a mill worker, and now a railroad builder. His parents died in one of the terrible forest fires of the 1870s, though. He doesn't talk about it much."

"The Irish I've known don't like to talk of past troubles," Veronica said. "Italians—well, they love to tell their tales. But I don't know how many of them are true." She chuckled as she said this. "We tend to be a nation of tale-bearers."

"I wish John would tell our children some of his stories," I said. "But he shakes his head and says, 'It's better if they don't know. They should have lives of their own and not carry their ancestors' burdens.'"

"I can see why he would feel that way, Mary."

'But people need to know what happened in the past in order to make the world better.' The voice in my head was back.

Emilia! You're still with me? I haven't heard from you in so long.

Veronica must have noticed a strange look on my face as these thoughts popped into my head. "Is something wrong, Mary?"

"Oh, no. I just remembered that I need to start John's supper. I promised him a special Irish dish tonight, colcannon."

"What's that?"

"It's made of mashed potatoes, cabbage, and milk."

She wrinkled her nose. "I'm not sure it would go well with Italian tastes."

"Ah, well, every man to his taste," I smiled. "I'd better get going. The cabbage must cook long enough to blend well with the potatoes."

As I began to walk away, a sudden sharp pain lanced across my back. Then, the pain moved around to my belly, and I gasped.

"Mary, are you having labor pains?"

"N-no," I managed to say. "I'm not due for three more weeks. This is just from moving too fast."

She walked beside me as I headed toward our shanty. "Well, if you need me, send Johnnie," she said. "This is your third child and may come early."

I nodded as I slipped inside the shanty door, closing it quickly. Then I cracked the door open and said, "Thank you, Veronica. But, really, I'm okay."

Slowly, I moved to the little kitchen counter and began chopping the cabbage. The pain ebbed and flowed as I managed to get the cabbage into a pot of hot water.

"Johnnie," I called, "Come watch this pot for me. The fire is warm enough, but keep stirring so it doesn't boil over."

My son climbed onto a stool and began to stir the pot.

Another sharp pain shot from my back around my belly, and I collapsed onto a kitchen chair beside our little dining table. Breathing in and out as slowly as I could, I waited out the pain. The next one came about six minutes later.

Emilia, what should I do? I never had my other two babies this early.

'When the next contraction comes, blow out puffs of air as fast as you can. That will help you through the discomfort.'

I did as she said, and this did help lessen the pain. The contractions continued to be about the same length of time apart.

You're doing fine, Mary. The main thing is not to panic.

'Not panic? My heart is racing. John won't be home for hours. I need to be peeling potatoes.'

Do you think you can stand?

I tried to get on my feet, but my legs felt like jelly. *No.*

'Then stay where you are. Where is Clara?'

She's taking a nap behind the curtain that hides our bedroom.

'Tell Johnnie to wake her.'

Another contraction began, and this one was the strongest so far. Then, I felt the liquid begin to seep from my womb. *My water has broken, Emilia.*

'Get Clara up right now. Tell her to run to Veronica's. She knows the way, doesn't she?'

I don't know.

'Then send Johnnie. Forget the cabbage. Dinner will have to take care of itself.'

I gasped as another pain shot through me only a couple of moments later. "Johnnie, go get Veronica!" I cried.

He stared at me wide-eyed for a minute, then jumped from the stool and ran out the door. By the time he and Veronica burst back into the shanty, I had fallen from the chair and was writhing in agony on the floor. Somehow, Veronica got me onto my back and bent my knees up. I felt her pressing my belly, and then everything around me turned gray.

The next thing I heard was her crying, "Push, Mary, push!"

Darkness threatened to take me out again, but I did my best to remember what it had felt like pushing when Clara was born. This time, it was almost over before I realized it. And then I did faint.

The familiar amber light from Emilia was the first thing I became aware of after my faint. 'Don't give up on me, Mary' came her voice in her mind. 'You have to live. Your new daughter needs you.'

A new daughter? Is she alive then?

'Very much so. Please, Mary, stay with me. This baby is my grandmother. If she dies, I will never be born.'

Die? No she mustn't die. I realized then that I was no longer on the floor. Somehow, Veronica and Johnnie had gotten me onto the bed. I managed to raise an arm and felt Veronica take my hand. Then she guided it to a small form lying on my chest. Tiny breaths lifted the baby's back. I felt a fluttering heartbeat. *Calm down, little one, Mama is here. I won't let you die.*

I rubbed in slow, gentle circles on the soft little back. The heartbeats became more regular. Then, at last, there came a little cry. A tiny hand began to grasp at one of my breasts. I pulled her closer so she was nestled between them. Soft little breaths felt warm against my bosom, and then her tiny mouth found a nipple and began to suck.

* * *

When I woke, Johnnie and Clara were staring at me. The baby was still nuzzling at my breast, but now her lips were just moving in sleep.

"Mama, are you all right?" asked Johnnie.

"Oh, yes, dear. You have witnessed something few men do. Not even your Da. But everything is fine now. Why don't you sit on the step and watch for Da to get home? Tell him I'm sorry that I couldn't fix his supper."

"Not to worry about that," came Veronica's voice. "I have peeled and mashed your potatoes and mixed it with the cabbage the way Johnnie told me. I think I'm the first Italian in history to make colcannon."

You must have helped, Emilia, I said in my mind.

'Oh, I had to give Johnnie a few hints, but not many. He's a sharp boy.'

"Have you decided on a name?" came a voice from the door.

"John! How did you get here so fast?" I breathed.

"I've been here since she was first born. Our brave son ran and told the foreman his mother was having a baby, and he let me off early."

Now I know how they got me into the bed. John was here. Is this another of your little miracles, Emilia?

'No this was all Johnnie. And the foreman does have a heart. He saw the panic in the boy's face and sent his father back with him right away.'

My husband was at my side, holding my hand now. "She is a tiny one," he whispered.

"She will be fine. I just know somehow." *Right, Emilia?*

'Correct.'

"Well, perhaps we should name her for her brave mother," said John. "Mary is a very blessed name."

"All right," I said. "Mary, it is, Mary Emilia."

"Emilia? Where did you get that name?" he asked.

"Oh, I'm not sure." I knew I lied. "But I think it has a beautiful sound, don't you?"

"Mary Emilia Cantlon," he murmured. "Yes, it is beautiful.."

"In my grandparents' country, the name Emilia means a diligent one, a hard worker," said Veronica.

"Then it's perfect for this babe," I smiled. "For she worked very hard to be born, even when I had too little energy to help her."

CHAPTER 24

From Iron to Copper

In the fall of 1890, our poor old mare died. I found her one morning lying in the little stall we'd built for her behind our shanty. It was a cold morning, and at first, I thought she was sleeping, but I pulled up an eyelid and could tell right away that there was no life left in her.

John was at work on the railroad, so Johnnie and I had to find a way to bury her. The ground wasn't frozen yet, so we dug a shallow grave around where she lay. Then we pulled down the stable's roof, put the poles that had held it up across the top of her body, and covered it with more dirt. We hoped this would keep the winter's wolves from digging her up.

We never found out, though. John was sent home early from work that day with his thumb swollen to twice its size and all black and blue.

"What happened?" I gasped.

"Stupid hammer-man hit my thumb instead of the spike I was holding for him."

I soaked his hand in cold water first to bring down the swelling. He was still in great pain, so I switched to hot compresses. These were folded pieces of scrap cloth, which I wet and warmed on the woodstove.

Neither of us mentioned our fears. If he couldn't work, there would be no pay. What could we do now? When he fell asleep that night, I sat on the kitchen stool with the Bible on my lap that Marie had given me back in the lumber camp. I tried to find something to reassure me of God's care—that He would somehow help us. My mind kept wandering to Marie as I scanned the pages. Where was she now? Was God taking care of her?

Then I came across a story Jesus told a crowd of people. He reminded them that God provided food for the little sparrows so that he would take care of his human children too. The thought of having enough food was marred by thinking of what had happened to John's people in Ireland during the Famine. But somehow, God had at least saved him and his parents. I closed my eyes and prayed, "Lord God, please take care of us like you do the sparrows."

I suppose it was an answer to my prayer that John's thumb wasn't broken, though it healed a bit crooked, and he couldn't bend the top knuckle anymore. This meant his work on the railroad was done. But within a few weeks, the line to Marquette was finally finished. This was a route for trains to bring iron ore to the Marquette harbor, where it was loaded on ships to be taken to steel mills in Cleveland, Ohio, Chicago, Illinois, and Gary, Indiana. Some went even as far as Pittsburg, Pennsylvania. There were many coal and limestone mines in those lower Lake States, two essential elements needed to process the iron ore.

The most blessed thing, however, was all the railroad workers were allowed to ride the trains going to Marquette. After eight years of wandering and working our way from the Soo, we finally made it to Marquette.

John got a job as a dockworker, loading the ore onto the ships. Once the winter was over, Lake Superior was safe to sail. But with his thumb injury, this didn't last long. One day, his hand slipped, and his arm was pinched between the ore cart and the ship's rail. Again, he was sent home from work, this time with a badly crushed arm.

When I saw him coming up the path to the little shanty we'd managed to rent, tears sprang to my eyes. "Not again, Lord," I murmured to myself.

John grimaced and walked up to me, holding his left elbow with his right hand. "Damn Cousin Jack called me a clumsy Irishman," he snapped.

"Cousin Jack?"

"That's what we call those Cornishmen from the southwest of England. They're Celts like us, but they believe in the Union Jack, the United Kingdom of England, Scotland, Wales, and Ireland. Damn them! To think they let the English try to starve the Irish into extinction."

I stood in shock at the anger in his voice, for I'd never heard my husband swear like this.

When he saw my face, he blushed. "I'm sorry, Mary. It's my pain talking." I saw a glint in the corner of one of his eyes and wondered if it was a tear of pain or frustration.

I did not comment and guided him into the shanty door with an arm around his waist. Again, I used the cold water soak in our laundry tub to help with the swelling. Then, I made warm compresses and made him lie on the bed.

"The work here is hard," he sighed at last. "I've heard that conditions for the workers are better up in the Copper Country than here in the Iron Range. This part of Michigan is sparsely populated, and companies import most of the immigrant workers from central and eastern Europe now. The Cornish have been here the longest and have swelled heads. They look down on others, especially the Irish."

"But you're American now."

"It doesn't matter to them. The owners of the mines mostly live back East in their fine houses. They've made their fortunes on the backs of poor laborers like us."

"I've read in the newspaper that most crimes are committed by the Irish," I said. "But is it true?"

"I think not," he replied. "If it happens to be an Irishman, they make sure to say it. But if it's a Cousin Jack, that's never mentioned. I hear there are so many nationalities in the Copper Country that it's different there. The mine owners are still the rich ones, but they actually build small houses and towns for their workers, even churches and schools some say."

"Where is this Copper Country, John?"

"It's over a hundred miles, and there are hardly any roads. The only way to get there is on a steamer."

My heart sank. "You mean we'll have to find a way to buy passage on a ship to sail on Lake Superior?"

He nodded. "I'm not too keen on ships, but a Great Lakes steamer has to be better than the English Coffin Ship my parents and I sailed across the Atlantic."

"But this lake is so temperamental. I've heard others talk of it often."

"It's late spring now, Mary. It will be all right."

I didn't want to admit that I was afraid of boats. After all, he was the one who had survived crossing the stormy winter Atlantic, and my voyage had been on a much better ship than his. Instead, I said, "How will we raise the fare?"

"Well, I've been saving up. When the other fellows head for the saloons, I don't. I've set aside some from every paycheck."

I tried another tactic. "What about the unions? Aren't they working to get better conditions for the laborers here? I've heard some people talk of strikes, where people refuse to work until the owners give them better hours and safer working conditions."

"Mary, the strikes often turn violent. Managers bring in scabs to walk past the picket lines and replace the strikers. Many times, fighting breaks out, and people are injured and even killed."

"Why are people so heartless?"

"The managers have to earn more and more money to pay their investors back East."

"The ones who get rich on our labors."

"It's even worse here in Upper Michigan, Mary. All the mine owners have to do is recruit more poor immigrants back in the ports of Boston and New York. There are so many people coming from Europe now that they can always find men willing to work for less. The mines pay their way out here, though they take the cost of that fare out of the miners' pay. They set them up in a little house and command their gratitude and loyalty for these small favors. There are places out West where men only have to work an eight-hour day, but up here, it's ten hours and for lower pay."

"I wish we could go out West."

"I haven't saved enough for that, Mary. Besides, it's thousands of miles over the wildest country. Our only options are to stay here or take a steamer to Houghton."

"Houghton?"

"Yes, that's the port where the Copper Country starts, where the richest copper in the world is found. Almost all the copper used in America comes from there, a place called the Keweenaw Peninsula."

"And it's further north in Michigan? Are the winters long, like here?"

"Yes, and often worse. I'm told they measure the snow in feet, not inches."

I sat in silence for several minutes, trying to pray. At last, I touched John's good arm. "All right. It looks like our only choice is to go to this Keweenaw place."

We had been so absorbed in this conversation that I hadn't noticed Johnnie standing beside the curtain in the bedroom doorway. He held baby Mary in his arms, and Clara stood beside him.

When he noticed that I saw him, Johnnie spoke. "So we're going to sail on a ship? That will be exciting." His eyes were dancing.

Clara, however, was clutching his hand. "Will the ship sink, Ma?"

I rose and put my arms around her. "No, dear. The lake isn't as stormy in spring. God will take care of us. We must move on again."

"Will we ever have a place to call home?" Johnnie asked.

"Someday," I said, hoping I wasn't lying.

***

When John's arm was healed enough, he began walking the docks, looking for a steamer bound for Houghton. After a month, he finally found one we could afford, with room for the five of us.

We didn't have a lot of possessions to pack, but sadly, we had to leave the rocking chair and the cradle behind—the rest fit in two battered suitcases that I found at a pawn shop. Our hopes were high when our little ship, the *Autumn Leaf,* set out on a warm, sunny day. Two days into the voyage, a summer thunderstorm whipped up, tossing the ship over large white-crested waves. Clara and I were seasick. John cared for little Mary while I lay on a wooden berth, unable to move. Apparently, Johnnie had the stomach of a sailor, for the rolling waves didn't bother him.

After another two days, the waters calmed, and our trip was tolerable. I learned that calm waters on Lake Superior still had many waves, though. When we finally reached Portage Lake at Houghton, I swore I'd never set foot on a ship again.

Houghton turned out to be the richer town, and across the Portage River was the smaller town of Hancock, where most of the mineworkers lived. On the hills above the town rose the towering buildings of the Quincy Mine, which had been in operation for many years. There were shaft towers, stamping mills, loading docks, and tramway lines for hauling the rock taken from the mines. I found it all very confusing. We were told this was one of the richest copper mines in the world and the deepest.

At least, the story about having a place to live was true. As soon as John was hired by the Quincy, we were given a little house at a very low rent. The little kitchen had a sink with cold running water and a nice metal coal-burning cookstove. The bedroom was separated from the kitchen by an actual wall with a sturdy wooden door. Our monthly rent was two dollars since the house had two rooms.

At last, it seemed we'd found a real home. There was even a school for Johnnie to attend in town and, wonder of wonders, a Catholic church where we attended Mass each Sunday. John worked ten-hour days except Sundays, when everyone got a day off.

My heart was happy now that we'd left the logging camps and railroad works behind.

CHAPTER 25

A Home in the U.P.

Time passed more smoothly once we settled in our little house in Hancock. Because of his old injuries, John wasn't hired as a "skilled workman" to operate the drills in the mines. Drills were powered by hand and strong arms were needed to swing the hammers or a steady hand to hold the iron rod being driven into the rock—qualities John no longer possessed.

After the holes had been drilled, charges were placed in them and lit to blast the rock apart. Everyone took cover as the ore flew. Then came John's work as a trammer, loading a heavy metal cart full of the pieces. He had a couple of helpers, at least. Then they had to haul the heavy tramcar to the lift, where it was dumped into bins which would carry it to the surface. That much he could describe to me. But he also said that the trammer boss was often tough on them, claiming they hadn't loaded enough, even when the cart was full. Some days, he ordered them to push the iron cart back down the tracks to add more rock, calling them lazy louts.

John told me that once the ore was on the surface, it was loaded into train cars that took it to the stamping mill. There the ore was pounded to fine sand-sized pieces. Then these could be run through some kind of wash plant to separate the heavier copper from the grains of useless slag.

After we'd been there about five years, a pneumatic drill, that ran on steam power, was introduced. It was extremely heavy, and it took two men to move it from one drill site to the next. This two-man drill became the norm. By this time, Mary, age seven, and Clara, age ten, were attending school with Johnnie. It was such a joy to hear Mary learning to read. Clara had beautiful penmanship and loved to write stories.

Sometimes, after supper, she'd convince John to tell her about some of his adventures in the logging camps. I must admit that I was surprised at some of the things I heard, things he'd never told me about, near-accidents with falling trees and widow-makers. He never talked of his parents, though, or of Ireland. I knew these things were too painful to remember, and he didn't want to upset Clara with their gruesome realities.

Four more years passed and our children grew faster than I could have imagined. Clara had been helping with the cooking since she was nine, and Mary joined her in the little kitchen when she was eight. I taught them how to make the pasties, which the miners took in their lunch tins. I'd been told that the early Cornish miners' wives had brought the recipe from Cornwall. Inside a thick pastry crust were pieces of meat and vegetables in a rich sauce. Sometimes, it was made from leftover dinner, but other times, we cooked up the stew on top of the coal-burning stove.

"Yes, I don't care much for the attitudes of those bossy Cousin Jacks," John would say. "But their pasties are the ideal lunch for a hardworking man. It stays fairly warm in a tin lunchpail, but if it needs heating, you just set that pasty on a shovel and hold it over a candle. That warms it just right for a hearty hot meal down in the depths of the earth."

The copper market had ups and downs during those first nine years, but the company took care of us. A doctor came if one of us took ill. They also provided grocery stores where we could buy what food we needed and could afford.

One night, as I'd just gotten settled down beside John in our bed, Emilia again came into my mind.

'You seem more at peace now than I've ever known, Mary.'

This is so much better than the ups and downs of the lumbering or even the railroad. There the company bosses just worked us and left us to fend for ourselves.

'Yes, you are comfortable here in many ways, but you are totally dependent on the whims of the mine owners. Their only goal is to use the miners to make as much money for their New York investors as they can. The company owns everything, including the land your house is on, almost the whole town, in fact. In the grocery stores, they set the prices and take the money out of the workers' wages. There is no choice.'

That seems so unfair.

'The mine owners own you. Sometimes they seem to treat you well, but if the price of copper goes down, it's the miners' wages that drop, not the mines' profits. They run this town, the politicians, the newspapers, everything. But at least you have a decent house and some compensation if your husband is injured or killed. There are cave-ins, rock slides, fuses that seem to fail until a man goes to check and gets blown up when it goes off late.'

That makes me glad that John is a trammer instead of a driller, even though his pay is lower.

'Yes, there are advantages and disadvantages to everything.'

Listening to her talk like this began to make me feel uneasy. *Are you warning me of something bad to come, Emilia?*

'Not yet. But mining, like any other resource-withdrawing industry, can't last forever. There's only so much copper, iron, or coal in the ground. Eventually things will run out. History has shown this over and over.'

Oh, but surely not too soon. We've found a better life at last. I pray the Lord won't pull it away.

'Don't worry. What year is it now? 1900? A new century is starting. There will be so many changes between now and when I'm born that it would make your head spin. You will have a better life than your ancestors did.'

John's life here is hundreds of times better than what his parents had in Ireland.

'Yes, even despite the danger. To be honest, life is always a dangerous thing, and each of us is only on this earth for a short time, compared to the ages that have already gone by.'

But, Emilia, when our life here on this earth ends, we go to God's heaven, where life goes on forever.

'Indeed, that's true. And it's good to remind ourselves of that, isn't it, Mary?'

And I'm only thirty-six years old. I hope I have many more happy years to come.

'Though I am not allowed to tell you the future, Mary, I don't think you will have the kind of heartbreaks your husband has endured.'

Will he ever be able to get over them?

'I'm not in his mind, but I think some of the deepest scars have healed as he's aged.'

My goodness, John is fifty-six. I wonder how much longer his body can hold up to this mine work.

'Don't worry. Things will be all right in the end.'

As she said these words, her voice faded. I wondered if she was leaving me for good.

* * *

In 1900, Johnnie turned sixteen and finished school. He

then went straight to the Quincy Mine office and applied for a job. When he came back, he had a big smile on his face.

"I'm going to be a teen driller, Ma," he announced.

"What does that mean?"

"I'll be an apprentice to a drilling team. Once they say I'm ready, I can be part of my own team. Just think, Ma, I can bring home a dollar more a day than Da does."

"Well, don't boast to your father. You know he's doing his best. His bad arm and thumb kept him from being a drill man, you know."

He sobered. "Of course not, Ma. I'd never hurt Da's feelings. I know how hard he works for us. I'm just happy that I can work now, too. Just think, we might be able to buy new clothes for Clara and Mary or even a new dress for you."

"That's sweet of you to think of, son. But I'm fine with what I have. I don't imagine apprentices get full pay, do they?"

He looked down for a moment. "No. I'll get a dollar less than Da to start with. But I'll work hard and do my best to learn fast so I can help."

Having Johnnie in the mine was a mixed blessing. I didn't mind making two lunches, but the thought of him so far underground, close to where those explosives were being set, made me nervous.

He did work hard, though, as he'd promised, and by the time he was eighteen, he was a driller with full pay. At that time it was three dollars a day, which seemed like a fortune alongside John's two dollars. Now I could buy some of the better cuts of meat at the grocery for our supper and their pasties. The girls had better sandwiches to pack in their lunch pails for school, too. That year, Clara turned sixteen and finished school, as well. She found a job helping in a dress shop in Hancock, doing mending and alterations. The only sad part was that she didn't have as much time to write. But John seemed to have run out of stories to tell.

So, as we prepared to celebrate Christmas 1902, things seemed the best they'd ever been. Until New Year's Eve. At supper that night, Johnnie made an announcement.

"Da, Ma, I've decided to move to the copper mines in Butte, Montana."

I dropped my spoon on the floor. "Montana? That's another world away."

John looked into his son's eyes for several minutes before asking, "Why, son?"

"They pay good wages there. And miners only have to work eight-hour days instead of ten here. I can send you some of the extra money I make. You'll still have an income from me."

"Where is Montana?" asked Mary.

"Look at the map on the schoolroom wall, sis. It's far beyond here, way out west. Past Wisconsin, Minnesota, and North Dakota."

"Why would you want to go there?" I asked.

"American's future is in the West, Ma. It's the frontier."

"The Wild Frontier," said John, setting his fork down too hard. "I hear the miners aren't as well cared for there. You'll have to make your own way."

"Da, I can't stay on this little peninsula in Lake Superior all my life. I want to see more of the world. Many of the Irish here are heading for Butte."

A single tear escaped one of my eyes.

John stared at his plate for a long time. The girls were pretending to eat, but I could sense their tension. At last, John spoke, "Well, Johnnie, you are a man now and able to make your own decisions. Just do one thing for us, try to write now and then and tell us how you are doing."

It seemed as though the whole room sighed. "Of course I will, Da. I love you all very much." I saw him blink and wondered if a couple of tears glistened in his eyes.

"Remember what I've told you about being responsible," John added. "No wasting your pay on the booze and the women."

"Yes, Da. But a man needs to have a little fun now and then."

John glanced at the girls and saw them both looking down at their plates. "A good man like you deserves a good wife," he said. "I've been blessed with that. Oh, she's let me go to the saloon to hang out with the Hibernians because they're my people. But I've not been one of those Irishmen who drank away their pay or had to fight to show how great they were."

"Yes, John," I murmured. "You've set a good example. I pray Johnnie will follow that."

"I will, Ma. I promise."

CHAPTER 26
Endings and Beginnings

The new year roared in with a blizzard. John and Johnnie made their way to the mine entrance since the underground was sheltered from the storm. Mary's school was closed for a week, and Clara couldn't make it to the dress shop in the bitter cold and blinding snow. This gave the girls too much time alone with their thoughts.

I tried to keep my fears for Johnnie to myself, but I suppose they could see it in my eyes. Since we'd had a good crop of wild blueberries that fall, I busied myself making blueberry pies and muffins. Mary kept her nose in a book, and Clara used her time to write in a diary she'd begun keeping.

One morning, after the men had left for work and the breakfast things were cleaned and put away, Clara sat at the kitchen table and said, "You know, Ma, I'm going to be seventeen soon. I've met a nice young man who wants to court me."

"Oh, really? Who is he?"

"He's the son of the owner of the dress shop where I work. His name is Isaac Strauss."

My breath stopped, and then I sucked it in loudly. "Is this shopkeeper Jewish?"

"Yes, Ma. You know many of them are. But Isaac says it doesn't matter to him that I'm Catholic."

I sat down hard on the nearest wooden chair by the table. "Oh, dear. What will your father say?"

"Isaac has been afraid to ask Da, but I think I've finally convinced him."

I took two deep breaths and stared into my elder daughter's eyes. "Do you love this young man?"

"Oh I do, Ma. He's very intelligent and loves to read and write like I do. And he's very good with numbers. He will be a fine shopkeeper in his own right someday. I'm sorry, but I just can't bear the thought of marrying a miner and sending him underground into danger every day."

I turned to look at Mary, but her eyes were glued to the book she held in front of her face. She must have known her sister would bring this up, and she didn't want to get involved.

Then I looked back at Clara. "Well, this Isaac must come and ask your father's permission. And you must be an obedient daughter and accept what Da says."

She looked down at the floor so I couldn't see her eyes. "Yes, Ma."

The blizzard lifted the next day, and Johnnie announced he'd bought his train ticket to Chicago. "The tracks should be clear in two or three days, and then I'm going. From Chicago, I can get a train that will go all the way to Butte."

"That will be a long journey, son," said John as we sat at the supper table.

"Yes, you should take some food with you in case the train gets stuck by winter weather along the way."

"They sell food on the train, Ma."

"Yes, but you should save your money," said his father.

"And you never know if the train may get stuck for days by another blizzard. They might run out of food."

"Oh, all right."

"I'll pack you some pasties and a blueberry pie," I said.

Johnnie smiled. "Those will be wonderful, Ma. I just hope others on the train don't try to eat them for me. Your cooking is the best in the world, you know."

This comment brought a chuckle from John, and the tension in the room eased.

When Johnnie boarded the train two days later, my tears flowed like rain and froze on my cheeks in the winter chill. He gave me a hug that was much too short, but I didn't want to embarrass his manhood by clinging to him. John shook his hand and then put his arm across his shoulders. "Remember to write, Johneen," he said reverting to the Irish term of endearment.

Clara and Mary both came, giving their elder brother hugs and kisses. I saw Clara whisper in his ear and heard his quiet reply, "Yes, now it's your turn, sis. Good luck."

Mary said nothing and wiped tears as she stepped away.

Then he boarded the train, waving at us from one of the passenger car windows. The engine got up a head of steam, its whistle screeched, and then, with loud clangs and chugs, it pulled out of the station, heading for the bridge over the Portage River to Houghton.

My tears continued to flow, hot enough now to melt the frozen ones. *Will I ever see my son again?*

I'd hoped for an answer from Emilia, but there was only silence. Then I remembered that she'd said she couldn't tell me that future.

* * *

Another blizzard roared in a week after Johnnie left. We wondered if his train had encountered it but received no word from him.

"Don't worry, dear," John said. "Mail is often even slower than the trains. I'm sure he'll try to let us know when he arrives safely in Butte."

"If he arrives safely," I sighed.

My husband said no more but patted my back.

This blizzard was so blinding, and the winds were so cold that even the miners could not make it to the entrances for three days.

When the weather finally cleared it was a Sunday. As we came home from Mass, I saw a dark-haired young man standing beside our stoop.

"Isaac!" Clara called.

He turned and smiled at her. I saw warmth and affection in his dark eyes.

When we arrived at the steps that led to our door, John brushed aside the new snow that had accumulated during the short time we'd been gone. As he ascended to our door, Clara took her father's hand.

"Da, I'd like you to meet Isaac Strauss. He's my employer's son."

John nodded curtly but didn't speak.

"I'd like to speak with you, sir," said the young man.

"Well, come in out of the cold, Isaac," I said.

Once inside, John sat at the kitchen table and silently motioned for Isaac to sit across from him.

"W-well, sir," Isaac mumbled. Then he spoke up more. "I'd like permission to court your daughter, Clara."

I could see John's face flush red. "And by your name, I assume you are Jewish," he said at last.

"Yes, sir. But I love Clara, and I'd be willing to convert if you insist."

John's face began to clear. "Ah, well, that's a horse of a different color."

"Sir?" Isaac seemed confused.

"It's an old saying." John chuckled. "If you are willing to become a Catholic, then I see no harm in your courting my daughter, provided, of course, that you are an honest man."

"I am, sir. My father has made me his accountant in the store. He can vouch for my integrity. However, I should add that he is not as happy about my intention to convert. He's been a faithful Jew all his life. As for me, I think what matters most is honesty and love for one's fellow man."

"And for my daughter, I suppose?"

Now it was time for Isaac to blush. "Yes, sir. I truly love Clara. In fact, I hope to marry her."

John pushed his chair back from the table. "Let's wait on that for a bit, young man. I give you permission to court her, with proper chaperones, of course."

"Yes, sir. When I am here, you and your wife are welcome. And at my house, my parents have agreed, as well."

"Very well." John stood.

Isaac and Clara smiled at each other. I was most surprised when John took each of their right hands and joined them together with his work-roughened hands. "May God bless you. I hope your lives will not be as hard as mine has been. A man always hopes for a better life for his children." He stepped back and dropped his hands. "Isaac, as long as you are here, you might as well join us for Sunday dinner. You have no objection to beef stew, I hope?"

"No sir, I have no objection. I'm not as orthodox as my parents. I'd even be willing to try pork roast."

John broke into a broad laugh, and I smiled in relief.

As we lay in bed that night, he reached across and took my hand. "I pray Clara will be happy and well-cared for. Being married to a shopkeeper will be a much better life than what you've had with me."

"Oh, John, don't say that. You have given me the best life you could. We are finally settled in a home here in Hancock. Our daughter will probably be marrying a fine local man."

"And I pray our son will find his way in the world," sighed John. "I'd hoped he'd not be a miner. But it seems to be in his blood."

"Well, this is a better life than a lumberjack or a railroad builder."

"Or a tenant farmer in Ireland," whispered John.

It was the first time I'd heard him mention Ireland in a long time.

When Monday came, John went back to the Quincy Mine. It was sad to see him walking to work alone, without his son at his side. The third day he was back at work, something terrible happened. Just after noon, the mine whistles began to blow loud and long. They kept going and going. Everyone in the town knew there was an emergency somewhere in the mine.

Crowds gathered around the shafts' entrances. I knew John was working down Shaft Number Two, so I hurried there. Mary and Clara joined me there, both being allowed to leave school and work. A mine emergency affected us all.

We waited for what seemed like hours. Rumors flew of a cave-in or a fire in one of the shafts, but no one knew which one. Miners were being released from all the shaft entrances after an hour or two—all except Number Two. My heart pounded, for this meant the disaster must be here.

After another hour or so, dust-covered men began to

stagger out of the Number Two entrance. They were so covered with dust that it was hard to recognize any of them. I wrung my hands as I scanned the ragged group for John. Mary and Clara clung to me.

Then at last, I heard a familiar voice, "Mary!"

I stumbled and ran to the dust-covered man and pulled him to me. "Oh, John, it is really you?"

"Aye, 'tis myself."

"What happened?"

"There was a cave-in along the stope ahead of us. Billows of dust nearly choked us, but we were the lucky ones. Our group was able to grope our way through the blinding dust to the escape ladders. Those ahead of us—I don't know—some were probably buried and crushed by the rockfall."

The girls and I clung to him as we helped him make his way home, oblivious to the dust clinging to our clothes.

* * *

Several days later, the bodies of the dead were recovered, and a funeral was held. We had been to several funerals in Hancock. They were a regular event in Copper Country. But this one was especially heart-rending, for twenty men had died in that rockfall.

After the funeral, we sat around the kitchen table in silence for a long time. Then John reached over to Clara and took her hands in his. "You marry your young shopkeeper, my darling daughter," he said. "He will give you the life you deserve. Perhaps someday you can write a book about how life was up here in the Copper Country."

Tears were streaming down her cheek. "I'll do my best, Da."

Only a week later, Isaac and Clara were married in a simple ceremony with the justice of the peace. John and I acted as witnesses. Isaac's parents did not come, and I prayed that eventually, they would come to love Clara, even though she wasn't Jewish.

Ironically, a letter arrived from Butte, Montana, the very next day, the first one we'd gotten from our son. Johnnie talked of his new job as a driller. They were using one-man drills, he said. But he still had a helper when it came time to move the heavy machine to its next location.

By the look on John's face, I could see this worried him, for it meant Johnnie worked alone much of the time, and if something went wrong, there would be no one nearby to go for help.

I continued reading the letter aloud, for John still could not read very well. Then, I came to a part where our son said, "There's talk of a strike here soon. The union, which we all have joined, wants the one-man drill removed. They are working to create safer conditions for us in the mines. I hope it helps. Some of the old-timers have told me of the violence of past strikes. The mine managers bring in scabs (non-union labor) to cross our picket lines and work the tunnels. Strikers and scabs break into violent fights. There are a lot more guns out here in the West, and shots are often fired. Men are wounded and sometimes killed.

"I see now, Da, that the Keweenaw was a safer place for miners. The companies there do take better care of their workers than the mine owners here. Still, the pay here is better, and the hours are shorter. We work only forty hours a week. I wonder what it will be like when the union men come to your Copper Country and begin to organize. I hope it will be more peaceful than here."

"What else does he say?" John asked, when I stopped reading.

"That's all, I'm afraid. He must have run out of time to write more."

Mary sat with us at the table, for she'd just gotten home from school. She was sixteen now and would be finished with school in the spring.

"Da," she murmured. "I don't want to marry a miner."

John reached over and took her hand. "That's good."

"But I don't want to marry a shopkeeper, either. Perhaps I could become a teacher."

"Eventually, I hope you'll marry," I said.

"If I find the right man, I suppose I will."

My husband's next words almost sent me into shock.

"I'd like to go back to Ireland."

"To stay?"

"Oh, no. Just to visit the old place once again. My memories are vague since I was so young. But I have a feeling if I go to County Kerry, something will look familiar. And I'd like our Mary Emilia to see where her family roots came from. Once you are out of school, Mary, we will set out. By then I will have saved up enough for the train fare.

"Poor Ireland is still under England's thumb. Many risings against that domination have failed. But someday, I still believe she shall be free. *Erin go bragh.*"

"What does that mean, Da?"

"It means 'Ireland forever!' Mary Emilia," he smiled.

"I'd like to see Kerry, too, John," I said. "The only part of Ireland I saw was some of Country Down when we visited an aunt and uncle. And I saw the northeast coast when my family left Strathclyde to come to America."

"'Twill be a long trip, all the way to New York to sail back across the Atlantic. It took us so many years to work our way here," said John.

"But now there are more railroads. Travel will be much easier than it was when you were young."

"Aye. I feel 'tis something I need to do, as a way to bid farewell to my parents once and for all—"

His voice broke, and I reached up to pat his arm. "You must do it then, John."

"Yes, Da. I want to see your homeland," said Mary.

"And one more thing," said John. "When we come back, we're going to stay in lower Michigan. I've had enough of this north country. I hear there is good farmland down there. We will find something somehow, even if I have to start as a tenant. I'm getting too old for this life of mining—or even logging. Most of Michigan's forests are all logged over now anyway. I don't want to go west into Minnesota."

I could hardly believe my ears. "You mean after all this time, you want to be a farmer, after all?"

"Well, I hope to own my land and not be a tenant like my father was, my dears."

"I'm sure you will find a way, Da," said Mary. "You always have. We have good lives, thanks to your hard labors."

"Thank you, Mary Emilia." He smiled at our youngest daughter, our only child left at home. "Somehow, after all this time, I feel I owe it to my parents to do what they never could and make a living off the soil of the land."

EPILOGUE

The room whirled around me, and I felt nauseous. "Where am I? What's happening?" I had a strange, empty feeling. I was no longer 'within' Mary.

'It's okay, Emilia, I'm bringing you back across the GAP to your own time.'

Is that you, Cinda?

'None other.'

Why can't I see you? I was bathed in amber light and couldn't tell if I was in a room or floating in space.

'Just relax, Emilia.'

But what happens to the Cantlons? Is that all I get to know?

'You did what you were sent to do. You helped them get from famine-stricken Ireland to a better life in America.'

It was undoubtedly a long and circuitous journey. And poor Thomas and Maggie died in that awful fire.

'Yes,' came Cinda's voice more clearly now. 'But Johneen grew up into John Cantlon and passed a rich heritage on to his children.'

They went in many different directions, though. The family didn't stay together.

'That was how it was for many families in the early years of the United States, Emilia.'

Actually, families are often living in distant places now, too. We just have better communication. What is it like in your time, another fifty years in the future? What year is it then?

'I live in the 2080s, and it's similar in some ways, but you know I can't tell you details.'

Oh, yeah.

I found myself sitting on the edge of my own bed back home.

'But I can tell you things that have already happened in the past,' Cinda continued. 'For instance, John and Mary Cantlon, with their daughter Mary Emilia, go to Kerry. John discovers he does recognize some of the rugged coastlands where he and his neighbors gathered seaweed and oysters when there was little else to eat. His little clachan was located in a place called Ratass, Cloonalour. He was even able to find a record showing that his father Thomas was one of the tenants there.

'When they return, they take a train to Cleveland, where they board a steamer bound for Port Austin, Michigan. This is on a larger peninsula in the lower part of the state. It's called 'The Thumb' because of its shape. The soil is rich and good for farming corn, beans, and sugar beets. Mary meets and marries a young German farmer named Frederick Wilhelm Haas.'

That's my grandfather. I remember him.

'Yes, he takes on John Cantlon as a farmhand and later as a partner.'

So, John becomes a farmer and owns some land of his own?

'Yes.'

And I remember my grandmother, Mary Emilia, telling me about their trip to County Kerry. But what happens to the other children—Clara and Johnnie?

'Clara and Isaac stay in Hancock and run the dress shop for many years. When the copper industry finally shuts down, they make a living running a small souvenir shop. They have two children, and she died in 1971.

'The Keweenaw copper industry folds in the Great Depression of the 1930s. Even before this, though, many Irish left the Keweenaw and went west to the copper mines in Montana and Arizona. The Quincy Mine, called Old Reliable, holds on the longest in Michigan. It ends up drilling nine thousand feet down, the deepest mine ever, but the ore quality degrades, and it finally becomes uneconomical to mine anymore. I think they give tours of part of the mine to tourists now in your time.'

Remaining headquarters building of one of the copper companies in the Keweenaw. There are remains of many mines and towns scattered around the area. Part of it has now been designated a National Historic Site. (Photo taken by Paul Erler, August, 1994)

But perhaps I have cousins in Hancock, Cinda?
'You'll have to trace that yourself, Emilia. I don't know.'
Well, I've only been to the Keweenaw once, so I think I'll try to convince my husband that we need to take a trip there. It is an interesting place with a unique history, so I'd like to learn more about it. I also know that Ireland finally gained independence from England in 1921.
'Yes, and the Irish in Houghton County, Michigan, gather $6000 in relief money to send in 1921, after the Anglo-Irish War.'

That's a lot of money in 1921! And it was mostly the poor miners, wasn't it?

'Yes, mostly.'

What about Johnnie Cantlon, John and Mary's son?

'First of all, he was right about the labor unions trying to get a hold of the Keweenaw. In 1913, they started a strike—mostly for better hours and to stop the use of the one-man drill. But it ends in tragedy, as many innocent people are killed in the violence, much of it caused by Strike-breakers hired by the mine management. The Union Strike Fund runs out of money, and the miners must return to work. Eventually, the mines do give the workers eight-hour days and better pay, though.

Demonstration of the one-man drill on a tour of the Quincy Mine, Hancock, Michigan. This was one cause of miners' strikes for safer working conditions. (Photo taken by Paul Erler, 1994)

'Johnnie never marries. By 1916, he had been promoted to crew boss at the Granite Mountain Mine in Butte. Unfortunately, on June 8, 1917, a terrible fire broke out in the mine, and he was one of 168 men killed. It is still the greatest hard-rock mining disaster in United States history.'

Oh, how sad.

'Unfortunately, not every story can have a happy ending. But there is a life after death, Emilia.'

I know. In heaven.

'God gave me a tiny glimpse of it once.'

He did, Cinda? Really?

'Yes, I was getting ready for school one morning, and suddenly, it was like a door opened in the air in front of me. There was the most wondrous music I've ever heard, and millions of people rejoicing. I felt so happy I thought I would burst. It was indescribable, really. I've never been that full of pure joy before or ever since. And I know in my heart that it was real, not just an illusion.'

How can you know that?

'I can't explain. I just know. There is a passage in the book of Second Corinthians where St. Paul describes having a similar experience. If it's in the Bible, it must be real.'

Yes, I suppose so. The Bible is no ordinary book.

Now, I could make out the features of Cinda's face. 'My father, Evin, is a GAP-crosser, too,' she said. 'He has told me a few things about the futures he's seen. He can't tell me details, of course. But he does say that he and some of the other GAP-crossers were given a vision of the New Heaven and Earth that God will create when this old fallen world eventually ends.'

So there's reason to hope.

'Yes, God is love, so He can be trusted. He will keep the promises He's made to His people.'

I sighed and closed my eyes. *Sometimes, I have trouble hanging onto hope. Look at Ireland now; in 2022, a century after its independence, there are still some troubles in Ulster, the six counties that stayed with Great Britain. Do conflicts ever end? How can there be hope if troubles just go on and on?*

'Emilia, what you experienced in the lives of Maggie and Mary is similar to what I learned when I was in the lives of some of your husband's ancestors.'

What do you mean, Cinda?

'Those ancestors went through tough times and trials, too. Sometimes, they were sorely tempted to give up hope.'

Did Maggie give up hope? Is that why you and that Time Guardian took me away?

'Perhaps it had more to do with the Great Ontario Fire.'

Oh. If I'd been 'within' Maggie when she died, I would have died too.

'Yes,' said Cinda's voice. Then she went on: 'I remember one of my ancestors often said, "Where there's life, there's hope."'

Well, I have learned one important thing about this GAP-crossing, Cinda.

'What?'

Even though my troubles cause me much pain—like what happened when our son Tim came out as gay, and his marriage fell apart, and we were cut off from our grandchildren after that—I see that everyone has troubles in this world. If they can get through them with God's help, so can I.

'Jesus told his disciples, "In this world you will have trouble, but take heart. I have overcome the world.'

I remember reading that in the Book of John.

'Sometimes, it's difficult, maybe seeming impossible, but we must hang on to hope and never give up. Even if you can't feel it, hope is still there, Emilia. Just keep believing.'

Her voice was fading now. Those last words echoed in my mind: 'Keep believing…keep believing…'

And then there was silence, but not darkness. Somewhere, deep in my mind, I could still see a strange, bright ray of light.

As noted on the cover, *An Irish Odyssey* is a work of historical fiction. This is my second work in this genre, the first being *Voices in the Past.* That first book traces mostly the line of my father's German ancestors, who immigrated to this country in the 1860s from Denmark and Bavaria, and settled in Houston, Texas, where these two lines met, when my great-grandfather Philip Jacob Henry Feser married Sophia Elena Hinrichsen. I was fortunate in researching this book to find a lot of documents and family trees on Ancestry.com and Familysearch.org. In addition, there were still living members of the Feser descendants who were keepers of many of the family stories and old photos.

However, the case with my father's Irish ancestors on his mother's side was entirely different. I could find very few records about the Cantlons because they were Irish peasants, and none of the family members are still living. As far as I know, my father, who was an only child, had only two Cantlon cousins, One died in World War II, with no descendants, and the other I have not been able to trace. As a result, when I referred to my father's Cantlon relatives in *Voices in the Past*, I used a fictional name for the family, Kelly. Since I had used what few facts I knew about this family then—such as they settled on a farm in Illinois—in *Voices in the Past*, I decided to create an entirely different storyline for this book, *An Irish*

Odyssey. The only other things my dad ever told me about his mother's father, John Cantlon, was that his parents had come to America during the Irish Potato Famine, and that there was a rumor this Grandfather Cantlon had gone to Colorado at one time, to seek his fortune as a miner in Leadville.

Ironically, however, there is more historical fact about the Irish in *An Irish Odyssey*, because I did a lot of reading and research in order to present the events of the mid-1800s as accurately as possible, even though my story is fictional. I decided to use this opportunity to convey what the Irish actually suffered during the Potato Famine, or The Great Hunger, as they call it. In addition, I wanted to show other paths many Irish immigrants took, such as the large numbers who entered through Canada rather than the United States, for reasons described in this book. Also, having lived almost twenty years in Michigan and being familiar with the lumbering industry and the mining booms, especially in the Upper Peninsula, I wanted to relate how these affected the many Irish who moved into Michigan from Canada, as well as from the U.S.

Being married to a forester, and having graduated from forestry school myself, I was well aware of the negative impact of the effects of mass timber-harvest of the best of Michigan's lumber in the 1800s. Living in Montana for 26 years, I also saw the impact of copper mining in the Butte area, and so I wanted to relate how the copper mining in Upper Michigan affected that region.

Therefore, while this book is fictional, it is based as closely as I've been able to on historical facts. (The attached Bibliography shows that I have read quite a few historical accounts of the Potato Famine, the Lumber Boom, and the Copper Boom.)

One other thing of note is that the first two chapters of this book actually happened as described, when I first visited Ireland as a college student in the early 1970s, and when my husband and I visited Ireland again in 2022. The only thing I have changed is the main character's names.

In addition, I have used time-travel as a vehicle in this book, as I did in *Voices in the Past*, in order to make the events more real to twenty-first century readers, and to shed some light on political and economic events that were background causes of the characters' experiences, but were not understood by them at the time. In some ways, this has been my most difficult book to write because it describes many of the injustices inflicted on the Irish—in many ways parallel to injustice experienced by indigenous peoples here in the Americas, and in other parts of the world, where Imperialism and Colonialism ruled.

Now to what few facts I was able to find about the Cantlons. First of all, they were a small clan in Ireland, so even many Irish don't recognize the name as Irish. On Ancestry. com, I did find a record of a Thomas Cantlon who was a tenant farmer in County Kerry, Ireland in the 1800s. This agreed with a U.S. census record I found from 1860, which showed he had been born in Ireland, but the birthplace was partly smudged so it read ...erry. Further research determined that it was indeed Kerry, in the southwest of Ireland, and not Derry, which is Northern Ireland. Another source, a Facebook site on Irish ancestry, also indicated that Cantlon was more likely a name associated with Kerry. This census also showed that Thomas and his wife Margaret had three boys named, Thomas, Morgan, and John, plus a daughter named Margaret, nicknamed Maggie. I also found Maggie's marriage certificate, which again confirmed Thomas birthdate as around 1815, and his wife's around 1818, both in Ireland. This certificate also gave me Margaret's maiden name of Crimmons. In addition, it indicated that they were Catholic.

From this point on, however, I have fictionalized this family, so I could bring to life facts that I have learned about the Irish Diaspora. To start with, I had John born in Ireland because I wanted my great-grandfather to be the one who experienced the famine and the voyage as a young boy. So I reversed his birth order with Thomas. In addition, I had to manufacture death events and dates because I have no information about any of them except John. I also changed John's wife to Mary McLafferty, a fictional Scottish woman, and gave them only three children, instead of the five John and his actual wife Sarah Parrish had. John and Sarah's third child was named Mary Eloise Cantlon, and she was my father's mother. However, in this book I changed her middle name to Emilia, and had her born in Michigan, for literary reasons. (I'm writing historical fiction, after all.)

The real Mary Cantlon did marry a man of German descent, as presented in *Voices in the Past* (though in that book she was called Mary Kelly). Therefore, I also had her marry a German in this book. However, except for the first two generations, all my Cantlon family tree in this book is fictional. Some who have read my other books will recognize names in the more recent generations as characters in those works. I have lived with these characters in my mind for years, so I feel I know them. (In the spirit of Madeline L'Engle, I tend to draw my characters from family trees I've already developed.)

For the sake of some historical accuracy, I am including photos of some of my ancestors who inspired this book. In addition, like the main character in this book, my time-traveler

Emilia Parker, my goal is to make history come alive again—and try to make a difference.

Modern readers need to know what has happened in the past. As Mark Twain once said, "Those who fail to learn from the past are doomed to repeat it." Unfortunately, some of the events and attitudes presented in this book are still in evidence in our world today. My prayer is that this book might start at least a minor ripple in a different direction than our world appears to be going.

*This is a photo of the man I believe
is my Great-grandfather, John Cantlon*

*Mary E. Cantlon, my father's mother, and my grandmother.
Daughter of John Cantlon.*

Mary E. Cantlon in the 1910s

*R.J. Cantlon,
my father's cousin,
killed in WWII.*

*My Great-Uncle John Cantlon, Jr. with daughter
Katie, Dad's cousin.*

BIBLIOGRAPHY

Bartoletti, Susan Campbell, *Black Potatoes: The Story of the Great Irish Famine. 1845-1850.* 1982: Houghton Mifflin, Boston, MA.

Captivating History (No author name given), *The Peshtigo Fire of 1871.* 2020: Captivating History Books, Troutdale, OR.

Classen, Mikel B., *True Tales: The Forgotten History of Michigan's Upper Peninsula.* 2022: Modern History Press, Ann Arbor, MI.

Clayton, Matt, *Irish History: A Captivating Guide to the History of Ireland.* 2021: Captivating History E-books.

Commins, Pat & Rice, Elizabeth, *Irish Immigrants in Michigan: History in Stories.* 2021: The History Press, Charleston, SC.

Coogan, Tim Pat, *The Famine Plot: England's Role in Ireland's Greatest Tragedy.* 2021: Palgrave MacMillan, New York City.

Gallagher, Thomas, *Paddy's Lament: Ireland 1846-1847.* 1982: Harvest Books, Harcourt Brace & Co., London, New York City, San Diego, CA.

Grosfield, Lorrie P, *The Nutshell Legacy.* 2024: Self-published.

Irish Civil War: A History from Beginning to End. 2020: Hourly History.

Kelly, John, *The Graves Are Walking: The Great Irish Famine and the Saga of the Irish People.* 2012: Picador, New York City.

Laxton, Edward, *The Famine Ships: The Irish Exodus to America.* 1996: Henry Holt and Co., New York City.

Lehto, Steve, *Death's Door: The Truth Behind the Italian Hall Disaster and the Strike of 1913.*

Mass, Kelly, *The Irish Potato Famine: The Immigration, Genocide, and Deaths of Ireland.* 2021: Self-published, Kelly Mass.

Metress, Seamus & Eileen K., *Irish in Michigan: Discovering the Peoples of Michigan.* 2006: Michigan State University Press, East Lansing, MI.

Michigan Humanities, *Great Michigan Read Guide to The Women of Copper Country.* 2022: Michigan Humanities.org.

Murdoch, Angus, *Boom Copper: The Story of the First U.S. Mining Boom.* E-book, reprint of book published in 1945. Original publisher unknown.

O'Roark, Reverend John, *The History of the Great Irish Famine of 1847.* 1902: Publisher unknown. Read as an e-book republication.

Punke, Michael, *Fire and Brimstone: The North Butte Mining Disaster of 1917.* 2006: Hachette Books, New York, NY.

River, Charles, ed. *The Irish Potato Famine: The History & Legacy of the Mass Starvation in Ireland During the Nineteenth Century.* (Copyright date and publisher unknown).

Russell, Mary Doria, *The Women of Copper Country.* 2019, Atria, an Imprint of Simon & Schuster, New York City.

Taylor, Richard E., *Houghton County: 1870-1920.* 2006: Arcadia Publishing, Charleston, SC.

Thoene, Bodie & Brock. *Ashes of Remembrance: A Novel in the Galway Chronicles.* 1999: Thomas Nelson, Nashville, TN.

ABOUT THE AUTHOR

M.F. (Mary Frances) Erler is a retired music teacher, outdoor educator, and author of fiction and non-fiction. Her teaching career has spanned over 31 years, and she has been writing most of her life.

She enjoys public speaking and sharing her faith journey, and is an approved speaker for Women's Connections, a Stonecroft Ministry. She has been able to speak, to date, at several luncheons in Montana and North Dakota.

Her published works include a 7-book series, **Peaks at the Edge of the World**, which are sci-fi-/fantasy with underlying Christian meanings, in the spirit of C.S. Lewis, her inspiration. This series is appropriate for ages twelve and up. She has always been fascinated with the idea of Time Travel, and uses this device in many of her books.

Following these books are two adult-level standalones which deal with contemporary issues, such as divorce, mental illness, suicide, gender identity, teen pregnancy, and children with learning disabilities and emotional issues. These are titled, **Lauren's Dark Passage,** and **Far from Magnolia Drive.** Both published in 2023. These are her only two books, to date, that do not involve Time Travel.

Currently, her favorite projects are historical fiction, using contemporary time-travelers going into their ancestors' lives, to bring history alive for Twenty-first Century readers. The first one, published in 2021 is ***Voices in the Past***, based largely on stories she learned about her father's German and Danish ancestors. Her newest book, ***An Irish Odyssey***, uses information from her father's Irish ancestors, plus some of her own experiences in visiting Ireland, and a great deal of research into Irish history. Her goal with this book is to highlight the mistreatment of immigrants to America, over the course of this country's history, and how they have overcome these challenges—although our country still faces many controversial issues in the area of immigration.

Among her many hobbies, Erler especially enjoys travel. She has been to several countries, including China, New Zealand, Sweden, Denmark, Finland, Estonia, Russia, England, Scotland, Wales, Ireland, Northern Ireland, The Netherlands, Iceland, Germany, France, and Switzerland (so far) as well as all the provinces of Canada, Mexico, Jamaica, and 45 of the 50 States. Her favorite mode of travel is cruising, and she has called six states home in her life: Arkansas, Illinois, Colorado, Idaho, Michigan, and Montana.

She has a Bachelor of Science in Environmental Education and Biology from Colorado State University, and a Masters of Music Education from Concordia University-Chicago

Hobbies include reading, acrylic painting, singing, and playing several musical instruments. She and her husband have two adult children. All make their home in the northwest.

You are invited to connect with her at:

Email: mferler@peaksandbeyond.com
Blog: MFErler.Blogspot.com
Facebook: @MFErlerAuthorPage